THE BILLIONAIRE'S KISS

A SECOND CHANCE ROMANCE (IRRESISTIBLE BROTHERS 6)

SCARLETT KING
MICHELLE LOVE

CONTENTS

Blurb	1
1. Warner	2
2. Orla	10
3. Warner	19
4. Orla	27
5. Warner	35
6. Orla	43
7. Warner	51
8. Orla	59
9. Warner	67
10. Orla	75
11. Warner	83
12. Orla	91
13. Warner	99
14. Orla	107
15. Warner	116
16. Orla	121
17. Warner	126
18. Orla	131
19. Warner	136
20. Orla	142
21. Warner	147
22. Orla	152
23. Warner	157
24. Orla	162
25. Warner	167
26. Orla	173
27. Warner	177
28. Orla	181
29. Warner	186
30. Orla	191

31. Warner 196
Epilogue 201

Made in "The United States" by:

Scarlett King & Michelle Love

© Copyright 2021

ISBN: 978-1-64808-776-9

ALL RIGHTS RESERVED. No part of this publication may be reproduced or transmitted in any form whatsoever, electronic, or mechanical, including photocopying, recording, or by any informational storage or retrieval system without express written, dated and signed permission from the author

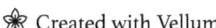 Created with Vellum

BLURB

Standing in a lobby full of people, bouncing auburn curls catch my eyes. As they slip through the crowd, green eyes peer out at me. My heart races, my body heats, and I can't stop looking into those eyes—they captivate me.

The relationship was doomed from the start. She's only here for a week. Long enough to have some fun—short enough for no real feelings to start taking form.

Or so I thought.

Our connection is intense. Our love, undeniable. Our ending, inevitable.

But she belongs with her family in Ireland. And I belong with mine in Texas. With a business to run, there's no way I can leave. With a family who needs her, there's no way she can stay.

But my heart still aches for her after so many months apart. And I have to wonder if hers aches for me as well.

Maybe there is a way for us to be together. I'm not an ignorant man. After all, I can think of some way for us to be together. Memories of her won't stop calling to me. I have to take a chance—for us.

1

WARNER

Whispers Resort bustled with activity as we celebrated the second anniversary of opening day. We'd awarded every guest who'd come the first day we were open with credit on every anniversary so they would return each year and join us to celebrate another year of success. And we had been extremely successful in our first year.

Along with celebrating, my brothers and I—the resort's owners—met annually to discuss what role each of us had played to help the business grow. Somehow, I'd made it last to the meeting in the main conference room where my four brothers had already congregated.

"Finally," my youngest brother, Stone, said as he took his seat at the round table, a cup of steaming coffee in one hand and a pastry in the other. "I'd like to get this over with."

Grabbing a coffee and donut for myself, I apologized, "Sorry about that. It's just that this place is hard to get around on days like this. There are people everywhere out there. It's insane." I took my seat as my brothers took theirs.

Baldwyn, the oldest, brought the meeting to order. "Patton,

you take the minutes." He pushed him the pad of papers and pencil as he was seated next to him.

We sat around the table in order of birth, which we'd chosen carefully to make us all feel like equals in the business. Baldwyn, Patton, me, Cohen, then Stone. As equals, we were to put in equal amounts of effort. And we all did—mostly.

As Patton jotted down our names, I began the process. "So, Baldwyn, can you tell us what you've done this past year to help grow Whispers Resort and Spa?"

"As you all know, it's my job to bring in guests from around the United States. I've gone to conventions in each state this year." He looked around the table at each one of us. "I've found that going to the conventions has increased what I like to refer to as our non-local clientele by twenty percent compared to our projections for our first year. As a matter of fact, I'd like to hold a hotel industry convention here sometime in the future. Do any of you agree or disagree with this idea?"

I was impressed. "I like the idea. Maybe we can hold a couple of conventions in the coming year. Like one for national hotels which you could head up. Then we could also do one for international hotels, and I could head up that one."

Cohen, Baldwyn, and I each held degrees in business management. Cohen's job was to oversee the entire resort and spa —he supervised all the department managers. When he heard my suggestion, his eyes turned bright with dollar signs. "Those two functions would bring in tons of revenue. I also like that idea."

Patton was an interior designer, and he too lit up like a sparkler on the fourth of July. "I could hold a convention for interior designers too."

Cohen liked what he heard and nodded with approval. "That makes three conventions in one year. I can almost already smell the money." He looked at Stone, who was gingerly stirring his coffee with a tiny straw. "How about a convention for chefs, Stone?"

"I don't care to head up anything like that. I prefer to *go* to the conventions, not *run* them." Stone was the laziest of all five of us. His one job was to oversee the managers of the restaurants, cafes, and bars we had at the resort.

Trying to entice him into doing a bit more than he usually did, I said, "You know, if you host a convention, you'll get to meet other chefs from around the world, and that just might inspire you. You should be cooking in this resort, not merely overseeing it." Stone was an amazing chef, if only he'd apply himself more.

Not bothering to even look at me, he simply shook his head. "Not yet, Warner. I'm only twenty-six. Give me some time to find my feet in the world of cooking, will ya?"

"You worked with chefs in Houston for nearly five years before we moved to Austin. Since we've been here, you haven't worked with anyone." I'd been silently noting his lack of enthusiasm since the move, and it had me worried. "Aren't you interested in cooking anymore?"

"I cook at home all the time. I cook for my friends often, Warner. I'm just trying to work out my own unique style before I ask for a restaurant here is all. I want it to be perfect, and I want the dishes I make to wow our guests. These things take time."

"Spoken like a true artist," Patton said as he shifted his eyes to me. "Warner, Stone and I don't think the same way you, Baldwyn, and Cohen do. Our work thrives on creativity, while you guys are rooted in numbers. He's doing well at handling the things he's taking care of right now. We don't need to push him."

He'd always taken up to defend our youngest brother, especially when he was slacking. "Okay, I'll let it go—for now." If I knew nothing else, I knew that Patton would defend Stone like a lioness defends her cubs.

Baldwyn moved the meeting on, asking me, "And how did you grow our business this last year, Warner?"

I was happy to make my report. "Well, I didn't attend conventions the way you did, big brother. I used the internet to reel in all the fish I've brought to our table. I've pulled in ten groups from Asian countries. I also brought in guests from Spain, Italy, and even India. At the moment, I'm corresponding with a group from Ireland. It's a large group, too. Twenty people from a town called Kenmare who want to pay a visit to our fair city, and they've expressed interest in staying at our resort while they're here."

"That's awesome," Cohen said with a smile. "It's good to see how our individual approaches have paid off. If we keep working like this, I see more resorts in our future."

"I agree," Baldwyn said.

Patton oversaw the spa side of the place. "I've brought in business for the spa through the internet as well." He held up one finger as an idea struck him. "Ah, we can add one more convention to the list, Cohen. How about a spa convention? That way, I could gain some more knowledge about the industry and make improvements to our facilities here."

"I think I've got my work cut out for me this coming year," Cohen said as he shook his head. "Well, at least that means we'll make even more profit next year."

We'd already paid our cousins from Carthage nearly half the money we'd borrowed from them to start the business. Within the next year or two, we would pay them off entirely. It felt good to be part of something successful. It felt good to be working with my brothers, too.

We were a tight bunch. Even though we didn't always agree or think alike, we still had a bond that seemed unbreakable. I suppose when you have no parents to make sure the family stays close, the children have to take it upon themselves to knit themselves together.

In the vein of keeping peace in the family, I asked Stone, "So, how about you make us dinner one night this coming week to show us how your menu ideas are coming along?"

My youngest brother's eyes lit up. "Really? You'd come to my place for dinner?"

I'd been over to Stone's new home only once, right after he'd moved in a year ago. We tended to gather at Baldwyn's house for most occasions. "I would." Looking at my brothers, I asked, "And how about you guys?"

They all nodded, so it seemed we were all in agreement.

"Maybe we've been neglecting our baby brother," I said to the group. "We should start going to his place at least once a month to try out any new dishes he's come up with. Maybe that will help keep the creative juices flowing."

"That would be awesome," Stone gushed. "I'm already thinking of at least three things I'd love for you all to try."

Patton bumped his shoulder against mine. "Great thinking, Warner."

Being smack dab in the middle of my four siblings, I'd grown accustomed to playing mediator within the group. Even when I'd been the one to start the trouble, it was usually me who figured out how to mend the fences between us. "I'll try to be more considerate of your artistic nature, Stone. You must forgive my business-first mindset. It can get in the way of what's really important at times. And you are what's really important to me, baby brother."

"You're important to me too, Warner." Stone's smile was as sincere as they came. "Thanks for bringing up the idea of me cooking for you guys. I hadn't even thought about it before, and the way it's already making me feel is beautiful."

Stone had always been a bit of a free-spirit—he would've fit right in with the hippies of the sixties. "Glad to help."

Baldwyn looked happy as he moved to the next order of business. "So, on to the coming year. How are we going to keep on improving? Patton, I'll start with you."

"It's obvious that the coming year will be an improvement if our convention idea is met with success. We'll all have to make a plan for the convention we'd like to host. Then, I'd say we hand them to Cohen so he can put dates on them since he knows best which times of the year are our busiest and which could work best for the conventions."

"I agree," I said quickly. "Cohen can take care of that. The sooner we have our plans set, the sooner he can schedule each convention and the sooner we can begin promoting them."

Baldwyn added, "We can each add all of the promotions to our usual marketing efforts. That way, there will be three salesmen for each convention."

Stone smiled. "Make that four salesmen. I've got a wicked following on social media where I can promote for you guys too."

I smiled at Stone. He was already engaging more with our ideas and plans—it was nice to see that all it took was a little encouragement and a request for a meal. "That sounds great, Stone. Thanks for the help, man." I loved it when we all came together to accomplish something.

"Yeah, no problem. Once you've got your marketing materials done, shoot them to me, and I'll relay them to my followers." He chewed on his lower lip as he seemed to be contemplating something. "You know what I just thought about?"

"What?" Baldwyn asked.

"Well, I have been putting up little bits here and there about the resort, and it got me wondering whether I may have been responsible for some of our sales and guests too." He looked at Cohen. "How can I tell if any of my followers visited the resort?"

"I'll hook that up for you," Cohen said. "It's not hard at all to set up data tracking with Google analytics. That way, you'll be able to give us some good numbers when we hold this meeting again next year."

"Cool. I like that idea," Stone nodded as he looked at me. "Who knows, this coming year might be my year, Warner."

"I hope it is." I truly did. Not that I wanted to push him, but I wanted to see him get excited about things again—especially his cooking.

I'd always envisioned him having a restaurant at the resort. Patton had the spa to keep him creative with the design. The rest of us had business to keep us occupied and working steadily. *Idle hands are the devil's playthings*, our mother always used to say. I tended to agree with her on that.

Stone had been a bit on the reclusive side since we'd come to Austin. I'd often worry that he was getting into things he shouldn't be. Many days he'd come in with sunglasses and keep them on throughout the entire day. If he could get excited about work and cooking, then I would be sure that whatever he was doing that wasn't healthy for him would end.

Baldwyn had always called me the mother hen due to the way I worried over my brothers. I was the one who didn't drink much. I was the one to turn down offers of cigars and other things people smoked. I was the one who looked after my health and made sure to drink lots of water. And I encouraged my brothers to do so as well, earning me my nickname.

Throughout the years, all my brothers had been hooked on one vice or another. Losing our parents at a young age took its toll on all of us. I seemed to be the only one who didn't turn to abusing anything to numb the pain.

But I did have my downfalls. I did have pain buried deep

inside me from the loss of my parents. Instead of turning *to* anything, I turned *away* from people fairly quickly.

One spat and I was often done with any girl I'd been seeing. Something kept me from getting too close to women. Probably the fear of losing them, but I never thought about it too much. Not that knowing that about myself fixed the problem anyway.

Since we'd begun working on the resort, I'd dated two women. One relationship lasted a couple of months before I ended it. The other lasted half a year before I walked away from her, leaving her in tears as she kept asking what she'd done wrong. I told her plainly that I was the problem, and I was sorry for the way I was.

A part of me must've been stunted after my parents passed in the house fire. I was thirteen at the time, and that year I had my very first girlfriend. Dana Caldwell was her name. We'd given each other our first kisses and thought we were in love.

With the death of my parents, I just shut down. Being kids, we drifted apart. And that's how my pretty much non-existent love life began.

I did wonder if a day would come when someone would light something up inside of me again. I was in my thirty-first year, and it seemed to me that fate had to have something in store for me. It just hadn't happened yet, but I wasn't getting any younger. I'd always thought that I would have found the right woman by the time I turned thirty. I had thought wrong, it seemed.

Despite my poor track record, I hadn't given up on love. But I wasn't exactly looking for it either. A part of me just assumed that something would fall into my lap, just as it had with the resort. Or better yet, *someone* would fall into my lap.

For now, I was content with having a successful career. A successful relationship wasn't within my grasp.

At least, not yet.

2

ORLA

"All I want to do is sleep the remainder of the day away so I can find out what this Austin nightlife is all about." I couldn't keep the excitement—or the exhaustion—out of my voice. Though I couldn't wait to start exploring, the nine-and-a-half-hour flight from Ireland to Texas had been brutal, leaving me jetlagged to the max.

The group I was traveling with was twenty strong, and it took two vans to take us from the airport to Whispers Resort and Spa in Austin, Texas. We'd traveled all night, arriving at our destination at ten in the morning. We were staying seven nights, and I hoped to have fun every single one of them. I'd worked my ass off for an entire year just to be able to afford a week's vacation.

They said everything was bigger in Texas, and I wanted to see that for myself. As we pulled up to the front entrance of the new resort, I couldn't even see the top of the building, it was so high. So far, Texas was living up to the hype.

We piled out of the vans, the majority of us still yawning and stretching, and porters came out in droves to unload our luggage, greeting us as they got straight to work. "Welcome to Whispers, y'all."

Moving with the crowd toward the double glass doors that slid open for us, I gazed at the lobby, as did everyone else. It was modern, stylish, and well-lit.

Working at a resort in Ireland myself, I loved visiting other resorts to see how mine compared. So far, this one was winning. But I wasn't ready to concede yet. To me, a great resort experience means getting along with the staff, so I was eager to see how friendly they were. Our staff was amazingly friendly and a real point of pride for me. I had my doubts about Americans being able to offer as high a standard of courtesy as we Irish did.

"Hello, Kenmare citizens," I heard a man call out. Though other people in my group were blocking my view of the new arrival, his deep voice reached all the way to the tips of my toes. "Welcome to Whispers Resort and Spa. I am Warner Nash, one of the owners of this fine place and the man who helped make your trip happen."

Craning my neck to see the man to whom the voice belonged —one so smooth and deep, with a touch of what I could only assume was a Texas accent—I caught a glimpse of him as he came our way.

He was easy on the eyes, standing at a bit over six feet, with his broad shoulders giving him a rather powerful appearance. Beneath his dark hair, which was short and neatly combed to the side with the part on the left, his clean-shaven face glowed under the enormous crystal chandelier that hung above us. A black suit, with matching matte black dress shoes and a pale blue button-down underneath the jacket, brought out the blue in his kind eyes.

Eyes that found mine. As soon as our gazes met, he zoomed in on me. "I hope your trip was a pleasant one."

As he looked at me, I slipped through the others to get to the front. "It wasn't too bad," I said with a grin.

"Glad to hear that, Miss—?" he asked for my name.

"Orla Quinn." He was so young and handsome, too. I was surprised to see he was so young, considering his relationship with this amazing place. "You said you're the owner here?" I blurted out.

"I am. My four brothers and I own this fine establishment," pride resonated in his smooth voice. Looking at him—listening to him—was an experience. It reminded me of the Jameson Bow Street 18 Years Irish whiskey.

As a barmaid, I often found myself thinking in terms of liquor. "But you're so young."

"Just turned thirty-one on the fifth of December last month," he said. "Nice of you to notice."

"Mind yourself, Orla," came the voice of Lilith O'Hare from behind me. "We're all ready to get to our rooms, girl."

The young owner's eyes were still on me. "I'll get out of your way so you can all check in and get to your rooms. If anyone would like a tour of this grand facility, I'll be in my office over there." He pointed to a grey door with his name on a brass plate at the top of it. "Feel free to stop by anytime you like."

I watched him walk away, biting my lower lip. I had just met the man, and he was already making things quiver within me. I liked it.

Wasting no time, I checked myself in, then headed to his office. He intrigued me to no end, and my feet wouldn't hear of going anywhere other than straight to him.

With a swift knock, I asked, "Can I come in?"

The door opened, and there he stood. Being that close to him allowed me to take in his height up close as he towered over my five-foot-five frame. I didn't want to have to crane my neck as I looked up at him, so I took a step back.

"Orla, right?" he asked with a smile. Perfect teeth, white as any pearl, gleamed against his lips. The lower one a bit plumper than the upper, his lips looked utterly kissable.

I had to stop looking at his mouth lest he thinks me a tramp, so I moved my eyes to his gorgeous blue ones. "Yes, Orla Quinn from Kenmare, County Kerry, Ireland. I work at a luxury resort and spa in Kenmare called Sheen Falls Lodge. I'm a barmaid at the Sheen Cocktail Bar. I'd love a tour of this grand hotel of yours, Mr. Nash."

"Mister?" Shaking his head, it was obvious he'd have none of that. "You call me Warner. You're not that much younger than I am. Or so I think."

"I'm twenty-seven. All four years separate us. I suppose I can call you by your first name, Warner." I couldn't recall ever being so drawn to someone. Looking over my shoulder, I saw the rest of my group heading to the elevators. "They're all too tired to take a tour right now." I'd been dreadfully tired upon arrival. But now that I'd met him, all that jetlag had somehow disappeared. "No need to wait."

Offering me his arm, he smiled as I looped mine through. "Then tour, we shall." Stepping away from his office, he said, "Ask me all the questions you want. I adore your accent, Orla."

"I find yours quite adorable as well." I'd always found it easy to talk to people, even if I'd just met them. I had to, working in the field I did—it made it impossible to be shy. "Do they call that a southern accent or a Texas accent?"

"It's distinctly Texan." He chuckled. "As Texans, we don't really cotton to being thrown in with all the rest of the southern states. We're kind of prideful in that way. How do things like that go in Ireland?"

"Kenmare is in Northern Ireland. There are many differences between us and those who call the Republic of Ireland their home," I informed him. "Our accents are different, as well. People from the Republic have what most people consider the quintessential Irish accent. In Northern Ireland, we've been influenced by the Irish, Scottish, and English, so our accents show that influence. And, of course, we think our accents are far better than those of the southern dwellers."

"Ah, so you can understand why Texans consider themselves a cut above the rest of the other southern states." Turning to take me down a long corridor, he went on, "This is the way to Whispers bar. So, tell me, what makes Northern Ireland different from the Republic of Ireland? Is there some sort of a border or something like that between the two?"

"Not a physical one. One of the things people who visit Ireland talk about is how they'll be motoring along and all the road signs are in kilometers. Then suddenly, the road signs change to miles. When you see those types of signs, it means you've entered Northern Ireland."

"That's how it is between the states here in America—aside from the change from metric to miles." He shook his head, contradicting his statement. "But there aren't any checkpoints the way there are when you cross into a new country. You just see a sign that says you're in another state, is all."

"But in America, you all use the same type of money, right?"

"We do."

"In the Republic, they use euros, and in Northern Ireland, we use pounds, as England does. It makes it a bit complicated for tourists."

"I bet it does." He pushed open a set of heavy wooden doors with etched glass at the top. One had *Whispers* written in green on it. Also in green letters, the other had the word *Bar*. "Here we are. Tell me what you think about the bar."

The room was full of natural lighting thanks to a wall of windows, making it feel nothing like the one I worked at. "This is different," I exclaimed. I was used to dimly lit bars with heavy, dark wooden accents. Here, the bar was made of white marble with pale grey streaks in it. The lights above it ran the entire length of the long bar, making it sparkle and shine. "It's appealing."

"I know it's not what most people are used to in a bar. We were going for something unique here. With the spa in mind, we wanted this bar to be airier and brighter than most bars."

The barstools looked comfortable, with dark grey leather covering the seats and a high back made of stainless steel for patrons to lean back against. "The seating is great. I love those comfy barstools and there's a nice intimacy to having those small sofas facing each other with a low table in between. It's like being at home."

"You have to see this place at night. We've got the coolest lights outside that bleed into the bar. It's like it's a completely different place."

"I *will* have to come see it tonight."

"Let me get you something to sip on while we take our tour." He walked up to the bartender and held up two fingers. "Can you get us two flutes of champagne, Gerald?"

"Of course I can, Warner."

"You come here a lot?" I asked as I took a seat at the bar.

"No. I'm not much of a drinker." He took the seat next to mine as the glasses were placed in front of us. Picking his up, he held it mid-air.

I took mine and held it up too. "What are we toasting, Warner?"

"To you having the best vacation ever, Orla Quinn." He clanked his glass against mine before taking a sip.

I sipped mine then put it back on the bar. "You certainly know how to treat your guests." I had the feeling that he might be the kind that picks out a woman in every large group that came in. "The women must love you."

Shrugging, he took another sip before putting his glass

down. "I don't know about that." His cell phone went off inside his jacket pocket, and he pulled it out. "It's my assistant." He swiped the screen. "Yes, Jezzy? Oh, I see. Yes, I'll come back right now." Putting the phone back into his pocket, he picked up his glass. "Seems some people in your group would like a tour after all. We'll have to go back to get them. Grab your drink and come with me."

Disappointment filled me as we left the bar to get the others. "I thought they were all tired," I mumbled.

"Guess they found some reserve of energy. Or maybe they were just more excited about seeing this place than taking a nap." His laughter echoed in the corridor as we walked at a fast pace.

"Seems so," I didn't even try to hide my disappointment. It felt nice being alone with him. And now I'd have to share him—and I didn't care for that at all.

As we walked back into the lobby, I saw Mona Pendragon with her mother, waiting for us. Cecil O'Conner and his wife, Angel, were there too.

I knew Mona well enough to know what she was up to. Warner's good looks hadn't passed unnoticed by her. The brunette had been hunting hard and heavy for a man she could call her own, and her efforts had only increased ever since she entered her thirties a few years ago. She waved, wiggling her fingers in the air. "Over here, Warner."

I waved back at her. "We see you, dear." Whispering, I leaned close to Warner, "Watch out for her, she's in heat."

A burst of laughter erupted from his lips as he looked at me. "Is she, now? Thanks for the warning."

Walking over to us, Mona extended her hand long before she was close enough to actually shake Warner's. "Mona Pendragon. Like King Arthur Pendragon. It's believed we're direct descendants."

Warner shook her hand politely. "Was he real? I was under the impression that he was just a character in a book written many centuries ago."

"Are you a scholar as well as a magnate?" Mona asked him, a slight frown on her pouting mouth.

"I wouldn't say so, but I *have* gone to college, and I *have* studied literature. But enough about me." He looked at the rest of the group as more people got off the elevator. "Will you be joining us on tour?" he asked them.

Nodding, six more people joined us, making us quite the bunch. "We should go before more show up," I muttered before taking a sip of champagne.

Mona's eyes were on my drink. "Oh, goody," she said with her shrill, nasally voice. "We get free drinks on this tour."

Suddenly, I didn't feel nearly as special as I had a few minutes before. The brochure had said the resort gave out free drinks to the guests, I remembered.

Given that I had a job similar to his, I should've known that Warner *had* to be nice to me. I thought that he might've had the hots for me, but nothing could've been further from the truth.

At least I had the alcohol to cool the embarrassment that swept through my body. "Back to the bar we go, then," I muttered under my breath.

Warner didn't offer me his arm this time. He led the pack back to the corridor as he rambled on about the tons of concrete that went into building the resort. And something was said about the zillions of lights that lit up the place.

I got lost in the back of the group as the jetlag came rushing back. As we neared the bar, I looked back, thinking about turning and going up to my room to take a nap. My feet kept shuffling forward though, as if they wanted to go on the tour that was no longer just for me.

A hand on my shoulder made my head turn back to the

front. There stood Warner, a smile on his handsome face. "How about you get behind the bar and make me one of your specialties?"

I smiled, thinking maybe I was getting the special treatment after all.

3

WARNER

Although she had to be tired after so many hours on a stuffy airplane, Orla's beauty seemed as if it couldn't be dimmed by anything. With a riot of auburn curls that cascaded down her back all the way to her waist, she walked in front of me towards the bar.

"Since we should all be going down for a nap soon so we can thoroughly enjoy our evening here, I'll make Celtic Twilights for everyone." Extending her hand to the bartender, she introduced herself. "Gerald, I'm Orla Quinn, a barmaid in Ireland. Would you allow me to come back there to make up some bevies?"

"It would be my pleasure," he said as he gestured for her to go back behind the bar with him. "I've never heard of a Celtic Twilight and would love to learn how to make them."

The way her sea-green eyes sparkled lit me up in ways nothing ever had. "Thank you, Gerald. Can you please line up rock glasses for everyone in the group?" She looked at me as she pulled out an apron from underneath the bar and began putting it on. "And don't leave Warner out."

Taking a seat on the stool in front of her, I couldn't wipe the smile off my face. "Definitely, don't leave me out."

"Would you like ice in these glasses, Orla?" Gerald asked as he finished setting the glasses on the bar for her.

"I would, Gerald. Crushed, please." She picked up a couple of bottles off the shelf. "You can use any Irish whiskey you'd like. I prefer using Bushmills for this cocktail. Can you pass me a jigger, please?"

Gerald handed it to her, then continued filling the glasses with ice. "Be sure to call out how much you use of the ingredients. My mind's like a steel trap. I'll be able to remember the recipe."

"Two ounces of Irish Whiskey," she murmured as she filled one end of the jigger. She poured the filled jigger into the bottom half of a shaker, then picked up the other bottle. "Two ounces of Bailey's Irish Cream." She filled the jigger, then dumped the liquid into the shaker too. Going back to the liquor shelves, she brought back one more bottle. "And one ounce of Frangelico hazelnut liqueur." She picked up the tongs and added four cubes of ice to the Boston shaker, then put the small metal tin over the pint-sized shaker and began shaking it.

The clanking of the ice made everyone stop what they were doing and turn their attention to Orla. I found myself liking the way her breasts moved beneath her cream-colored sweater as she shook the drink. "I can't wait to taste it."

Putting the shaker down, she picked up a strainer then pulled one of the ice-filled glasses towards her. "Using a Hawthorne strainer to keep the ice in while the creamy, smooth, and now cold cocktail pours out over the crushed ice, you have an authentic Irish cocktail, the Celtic Twilight, made by a real Irish lass." She pushed the short glass toward me with a wink. "Tell me what you think."

Picking it up, I inhaled the unique aroma of the whiskey, the hazelnut liqueur, and the cream before I took a sip. A flame of warmth washed through me as the cool drink slipped down my throat. My tongue was absolutely delighted with the mixture of flavors that teased my tastebuds. "Oh, Orla." I didn't know what to say as I took another sip. "Creamy, smooth, and so damn good it ought to be illegal. Great drink. Awesome drink."

"Would you like to try your hand at making one, Gerald?" She handed the bar back over to him. "I'll take your first one."

Rubbing his hands together, he looked eager. "I would love to make the rest of them so I can get this cocktail down."

Untying the apron she'd put on, she then folded it and put it back where she'd found it before taking a seat next to me. "That was fun. Thanks for letting me do that, Warner."

"Thanks for doing it." I took another sip. "This is really delicious."

"I thought you'd like it." She took the finished drink Gerald gave her and took a sip. "Ah, you did it perfectly, Gerald."

His eyes lit up at the compliment. "Thank you for showing me how to make it, Orla. You're a real pro."

"I'm sure you are too." She took another sip before saying, "I'll be here for a week. Perhaps I can come down during the days, and you can teach me how to make some of your Texas specialties, and I'll teach you more Irish ones."

"It's a deal." He smiled at me. "Thanks for bringing her to me, Warner. She's going have me upping my bartender game."

As long as that's the only game she'll be upping for you, my man.

"Glad it's working out for you both." It had been a long time since I'd found a woman so alluring and attractive in both personality and physical appearance.

But I had to remember that Orla would only be in town for seven nights. I'd never been the type of man who got right down to the nitty-gritty with any woman. I liked to take my time—get to know them a little—before I got into a sexual relationship with them. But with Orla, I didn't have the luxury of time. And the idea of letting her slip through my fingers, even if I could only hold her for a week, didn't sit well with me.

Plus, there was one great benefit of her leaving—it meant there would be no break-up. And that sounded amazing to me.

We'd simply kiss goodbye at the end of her stay, and then off she'd go, back to Ireland to live the rest of her life while I would do the same here in Texas. The most perfect relationship plan I'd never heard.

"Can I have the next one?" Mona asked Gerald. She took the seat on my other side. "So, Warner, we've heard tales of the wild Austin nightclub scene. Is it all just a bunch of Texas bragging, or are the rumors true?"

"It's true—and it's not called bragging if it's true." I took another sip of my drink, wishing like crazy that the others hadn't shown up, and crashed the intimate tour I had planned for Orla. "It's like they say—everything's bigger in Texas—and that applies to our nights out too. You'll find that we party harder than most."

"More than the Irish?" Mona's mother asked as she took the place on the other side of Mona.

I didn't want to offend any of them, so I kept my lips shut tightly. Orla laughed as she saw my reaction to the question. "The Irish do drink a lot. But I wouldn't say they're the best at partying. From what I've heard, Americans take partying to levels we can't even comprehend."

"I would like to give you all a bit of advice," I said. "Don't take any drugs anyone offers you. And don't leave the club with strangers, either. Have fun, drink all you want, dance with whoever you want, but get into the vans we provide and come back here with our drivers—alone. Don't bring some random back with you. God only knows what might happen to you."

"Aw," Orla said with a grin. "You're a mother hen, aren't you?"

"As a matter of fact, I have been called that from time to time. I just don't like to see people get hurt." I really didn't want to see anything bad happen to Orla—or any of the other guests. "Plus, we have a bit of nightlife here at our resort as well. The restaurants have live bands each night. Sometimes the bar does, too—on weekends mostly. You don't have to venture out to get a good taste of the Austin nightlife."

"You are a sweetie." Orla got up as the last drink was handed out. "Now that we're all armed with drinks, shall we get on with this tour? I'd love to see more."

"Oh, me too." Mona hopped off the barstool to flank me on one side while Orla flanked the other. Mona made a small huffing sound as if it miffed her that Orla had come along too.

The three of us couldn't all fit out the door at the same time, so I opened the door and let the two of them walk out first. Holding the door open for the others, I exited last. We'd be going out the side door to the garden patio, so I was now in the front of the group. "Okay, we're going to go out this door here. If you follow me, we can get this tour going again, starting with the garden."

Mona made such a loud huff—presumably at now being at the back of the line—that I almost laughed. Orla had been right, the girl *was* in heat, it seemed.

But my eyes weren't on Mona. I only had eyes for Orla, who smiled at me over the rim of her glass.

I had to turn around, pulling my gaze away from hers. She was mesmerizing me with such ease, it wasn't even fair. Not that I could let her know. Somehow, I would have to play it cool—that would be the best way to pull her towards me. When a woman took the first step, the game always went faster than if she had to be chased. At least that's what I'd seen happen with Cohen—the playboy among my brothers.

Cohen was smart in many ways. Business, of course, and a

lot of other areas. But his way with women was pure brilliance. Not that I'd ever overly thought about being able to get a woman into my bed as quickly as possible, as he liked to. But Orla was different. So I figured I'd borrow some tried and true moves that I was sure would work.

Moving the tour along fairly quickly without rushing it, I knew everyone had to be jetlagged and needed a good nap. "So, here we are in the lobby again. I would like to wish you all a good afternoon, and I look forward to seeing you around the resort this coming week."

Turning away from them, I headed to my office. As I left, I felt a pair of eyes on me, burning a hole in my back. I didn't turn around.

When a hand slipped down my arm, a chill ran through me. Not a good one, either.

"Warner," came Mona's high-pitched voice. "Where would you suggest my mother and I have dinner this evening?"

I had to turn around and give her my attention. And when I did, I saw Orla grinning at me, her lips curving only slightly as she shook her head. "You should check out the menus in your room. They show what food is served in each of our restaurants, all of which are amazing in their own way. I'm sure you'll find any one of them enjoyable."

"Where do *you* like to eat?" she asked with a lilt to her nasally voice. "Perhaps we could dine together this evening."

There was no way in hell I'd be dining with her. I hadn't ever dined with any of our guests, and I wasn't going to start with her. "I love all the places here at the resort. And unfortunately, I've already got dinner plans tonight. I'm sure you'll have a great experience, though."

"I suppose." She turned and walked away with her head down.

For a moment, I felt kind of bad. Not that I was going to

change my mind, but I did feel sorry for her. *Poor thing. She doesn't realize she just tries too damn hard.*

Orla raised a hand, waving at me. "Thanks for the tour, Warner." And then she turned and walked away.

I stood there, frozen, as I watched her leave the lobby and get into the elevator with the rest of her group. I waved, looking only at her, but out of my peripheral vision, I saw that some of them waved back at me. And then the elevator door closed, and I turned to go to my office.

I took a seat behind my desk and laid out my arms, folding them to create a pillow as I rested my head on top of them. I wasn't exactly sure why I felt so dreamy, like my head was floating on a cloud. I'd had two alcoholic drinks, so that might've enhanced the way I was feeling about Orla. Whatever it was, I liked it.

Knowing that she'd be leaving made it easy to let go of the usual fear I had in relationships—that I would lose her. I *knew* I would lose her. But my mind was occupied by the things we could do while I still had her. With other women, I usually spent far too much time thinking about all the what-ifs.

With Orla, there were no what-ifs. There were only facts. Like the fact that we had a spark. Like the fact that I couldn't find a thing about her that I didn't like. Like the fact that this would not last.

The lack of fear over the unknown was a huge pro as well as a huge relief. I'd always felt that fear with every woman I went out with since I was sixteen. But Orla didn't inspire any fear in me. She only inspired other things—arousing things.

I wanted to try new things with her. I'd already done something I'd never done before—drinking in the morning. What else would the lass inspire me to do?

All I knew was that I had to find out. I had to find out what her satin-smooth, alabaster skin felt like against mine. I had to feel her rosy red lips succumbing to mine. My fingers itched to tangle in her auburn curls. But first, I would have to play the game and get her to come to me. I couldn't get impatient, either. Somehow, I would have to play it cool, become a different kind of guy. The kind that women throw themselves at.

For the first time, I felt completely out of sorts about a woman. But if this feeling was wrong, then I didn't want to be right.

4

ORLA

My nap turned into an all-day event. I woke up just in time to see the sunset from the glass door on my balcony. Stretching, I couldn't stop gazing at the dizzying array of colors, the melting sun draped over the city. It was a blur of headlights, bright building lights, and streetlights that blazed their silver beams upon the remarkably still busy residents.

The phone in my room rang, startling me. "Feck me!" A red light notified me of the waiting caller, and I walked over to pick up the handset. "Orla here."

"We're going to dinner now, and Mother said I should ask you if you'd like to join us since you're a woman on your own," Mona said. "We're going to try the Mexican food at The Fiesta Room here at the resort."

"Spicy." I did want to try the Mexican—just not with those two. "My tummy's not up for that yet, but thanks anyway. You two have a nice time."

"Okay," she sounded relieved, but I heard her mother in the background, chastising her. "You are going to eat something, aren't you? Mum wants to make sure you eat."

"Tell her that I will certainly eat, and thanks for looking out for me. Mum and Pop will be glad she's doing it, too." I hung up the phone, wondering where that handsome hotel owner would be eating his dinner. "What are you up to, Warner Nash? I've little enough time to make you mine. At least, for the week."

I wasn't in America to find myself a mate for life. But a mate for a week didn't sound bad at all. And Warner just happened to check all my boyfriend boxes. Tall, dark, handsome, witty, and generous—the most important things to me in a man. Good looks alone merely weren't enough. I'd found that out the hard way.

In my line of work, I'd met many, many men. And my eyes, like most people's would, found themselves falling upon the handsomest. I'd dated a few of them in my time. And out of these few, only one had a decent personality; the others seemed to be coasting by on their looks.

The other problem with dating attractive men is that other women also found them irresistible. That's precisely how I'd lost the one gorgeous man who did have a worthwhile personality—a daring lass had presented herself as another option. I chalked it up to the fact that he must've never been mine, or he wouldn't have responded to Sarah Gallagher's slithering tongue in the first place.

With the night ahead at the forefront of my mind, I went to shower and get ready. An hour later, I was standing in front of the full-length mirror, rotating to check out my backside. "Perky." I shook my bottom, making the flowing dress move like waves around my ankles. Being January, it was far too cold to wear anything more revealing, I thought.

Looking up, I closed my eyes. *I'm opening myself up to you fate—let's see what you have in store for me.*

Walking out the door, I found Mr. and Mrs. Maguire walking hand in hand down the hallway. "Evening," I greeted them.

"Good evening, Orla," Mrs. Maguire said with a nod. "We're

going to meet with the Walsh family at the restaurant called Essence. Would you care to join us? It sounds like a steakhouse—lots of meat and seafood on the menu."

"That sounds nice, thank you." Walking alongside them, I reflected on how much I loved taking vacations in groups from our town. It made traveling so much easier and less stressful. "Sounds like something Mum and Pop would like. They wanted to come on the trip too, but Pop threw his back out and they had to sell their tickets to the McCarthys."

"Well, you've got your extended family of Kenmare citizens here with you, Orla," Mr. Maguire said with sincerity. "You don't need an invitation to join us for anything, you know."

"That's very nice of you. I do appreciate that." Vacationing with my parents was nice, but it had made it impossible for me to ever have the romantic vacation fling I'd dreamed of having for ages. Not that I was sure this would be one of those dream vacations, but at least I was free if it did come my way.

Getting into the elevator, it took us to the very top of the building. When we stepped off, we were at the entrance to a restaurant that sparkled from within, already filled with people.

The sounds of jovial conversations replete with laughter formed a smile on my lips. The chatter was contagious, and I knew that whatever happened tonight would, at the very least, make me laugh. "Sounds fun in there, doesn't it?"

"It surely does," Mrs. Maguire agreed as she, too, was wearing a broad smile. "Come, let's get inside and join the fun."

As we stepped up to the hostess station, Mr. Maguire spotted the rest of our party. "Oh, I see Byron. Seems they've already gotten a table. Lucky for us, it has three more free places. I didn't anticipate this crowd."

The hostess took us to join the others. I ran my hand over the bright red curls of twelve-year-old Jason Walsh as I walked behind him. "Evening, Jason."

"Oh, good. I'm glad you're joining us, Orla. I was afraid I was going to be the fifth wheel here tonight." He jumped up and pulled out the empty chair beside him. "Please, sit by me."

Taking the seat, I thought about what a fine young gentleman he already was. "Thank you, Jason." I turned to his parents, giving them a nod. "You're doing a good job with this one, I must say."

"Thank you," Mrs. Walsh said with a proud smile. "He's our pride and joy."

Jason bumped his shoulder against mine as I picked up the menu. "What do you say to sharing a cocktail with me, Orla?"

I had to laugh. "I'll do it."

"You will?" he asked with surprise.

"Sure. When you turn eighteen, I'd love to share a cocktail with you." I tweaked his nose, then looked at the menu. "What are you going to have for dinner, Jason?"

"Steak and lobster."

I thought that was a rather large meal for such a thin boy. "Both? How about I order the lobster, and you order the steak, and we can share?"

"I like that idea," his father said. "I know he won't be able to eat all of that food."

"Deal," Jason agreed. "And we can share a dessert, too. There are so many of them, and they all look so good."

"Choose one, and I'll share it with you. I'm not picky. If it's sweet, I *will* eat it." I searched for what would pair well with both meat and seafood from the beverage section. "There's something called sweet tea." I looked at the others at the table. "Any idea what that is?"

"Ask the waiter," Mrs. Walsh answered. "I know they make some mixed drinks they call teas, but they're anything but tea."

"Ah, like the Long Island iced tea. Yes, I'll have to ask." Putting the menu down, I caught someone moving out of the corner of my eye and turned to find Warner Nash walking along the far side of the room. Our eyes met, and he raised his hand, waving at me.

Please come over here to say hello.

But he didn't come to me at all. Instead, he kept walking all the way to the back of the room, where there was a small bar with only a handful of seats. It wasn't meant to be a bar that people hang out at. It was primarily for making the cocktails that were served with the meals. But Warner took a seat and began talking to the bartender, who was quick to place a pint of beer in front of him.

The waitress came to our table and interrupted my spying of the man, who I couldn't stop trying to sort out. One moment I felt that he was attracted to me, the next I felt like a fool for thinking that way. And here I was again, feeling foolish.

"Are y'all ready to order?" the waitress asked with a strong Texas accent.

"I have a question," I said, grabbing her attention. "What is in the sweet tea?"

She looked at me in bewilderment with eyes that didn't blink. "Well, there's tea and sugar and ice in that."

"It's not a cocktail?" I didn't understand this sweet tea thing at all.

"There's no alcohol in it. But it's really good," she said. "It's a southern specialty. In Texas and most of the south, you'll find it in just about every home, restaurant, cafe, and pretty much anywhere you can get food."

"Well, I'd like to give it a try, then. And for food, I'll have the lobster with zucchini and mashed potatoes."

I zoned out as the others made their orders, staring a hole into Warner's back, hoping he'd turn and see me. Not that I knew what I would do if he did. But I just wanted him to show me some attention, the way he'd done when I first arrived in the lobby that morning. His eyes had been glued to mine then.

Even though the company was nice and the food was too, I found myself a bit on the absentminded side as I kept stealing glances at Warner. Once we'd all finished our meals and everyone got up to leave, I bid my companions good night and made my way to the bar in the back of the room.

Taking the seat at the opposite end of the bar from Warner, I pretended not to notice him. "I'd like to try your best Texas cocktail, please. What do you recommend?"

"You want sweet or bitter?" the bartender asked.

"Sweet."

"How about the Texas buck? It's got whiskey, honey, and ginger beer with a candied ginger garnish."

"Sounds good. I'll give that a try."

"It is good." Warner slid onto the stool next to mine. "Did you enjoy dinner?"

"I did." *And I'm enjoying you finally talking to me even more.*

"You'll have to forgive me for not coming to say hello. I didn't want to interrupt."

"Forgiven." I took the drink the bartender placed in front of me and took a sip, feeling much better now that I had Warner's attention. "This is amazing."

"Thanks," the bartender said before he left us, busying himself with other drink orders.

"So, Ireland," Warner said. "What's it like to live there?"

"That's a broad question and one that can't be answered in a line or two." I took another sip. "It feels sort of small sometimes—especially in our town. I inherited my grandparent's cottage two years ago, which is a nice, tiny place. It's so tiny that I find it hard to believe they raised five children there, especially with only two bedrooms and one bathroom. But they did."

"So, you like it? Or not so much?" he asked as he leaned his elbow on the bar, resting his cheek on the palm of one hand.

"I love it." I couldn't believe they'd left it to me. "I've got more cousins than I can count. It was a true privilege to have that place. There are rose bushes by the front door that are ancient. And there are so many things about the house that make it very special to me."

"Sounds like it's a place you'll never want to leave."

"I know that I don't want to leave it right now. Who knows about the future, though? If I ever do marry and have children, I know it'll be too small for an entire family."

"So, I take that to mean you're single? The right man hasn't swept you off your feet?" he asked with a sexy grin that melted things inside of me that had never melted before.

"Not yet." I took another sip to slow the burn between my thighs.

"Good." He laughed. "I mean, for me." His eyes drifted to the bar, and then he looked back at me. "Not that I'm trying to hit on you."

"It doesn't seem like you're *trying* at all. It's coming quite naturally to you," I teased him.

Moving one hand, he grabbed a lock of my hair and twirled it around one finger. "You must be used to this kind of thing—it must happen all the time to a woman as gorgeous as you."

"You'd be surprised how often this does *not* happen to me." I could feel my cheeks blushing at his compliment—a very rare occurrence for me. "And I'm cute, but that's about it. Gorgeous is a bit too much."

"You *are* gorgeous." His hand slipped away from me to rest on his thigh. "I think you're very brave, you know."

"Why is that?" I sipped my drink again, liking the way he looked at me with a soft gaze.

"Coming to a foreign country all alone. Was your family worried about you traveling on your own?"

"I'm not alone. I'm with a group a people I've known most of my life. And my parents were supposed to come, but my father threw out his back. Otherwise, I wouldn't be sitting here talking to you; my father wouldn't have allowed that to happen."

"Lucky me again." He chuckled, the deep sound penetrating my ears so soothingly. "Is this what they call the luck of the Irish?"

"I don't think so. But I do feel a bit of luck myself. I'm twenty-seven, and this is the first vacation I've been able to take without my parents guarding me like some precious stone."

"Ah. And have they gotten in the way of your dating life back home as well?" Something danced in his blue eyes.

"I've had boyfriends, Warner, if that's what you're asking. It's a bit different when we're traveling out of the country, though—they don't want someone stealing me away to some foreign land. Apparently, as long as a lad is Irish, then that's all they care about."

"So they wouldn't approve of you marrying an American?" he asked.

I'd just taken a sip and nearly spit it right back out. "Who said anything about marriage?"

"Sorry," he said with a laugh. "Not that I'm proposing. I was just asking if they would approve of a thing like that."

"I have no idea. They're not prejudiced people. They're just wary of others when traveling abroad. As long as they got a chance to get to know this hypothetical American man who wanted to marry me, then I'm sure they'd approve."

This is some sort of record, talking about marriage before we've even kissed.

5

WARNER

What was I thinking, bringing up marriage? Better get away from the subject before I scare her away.

"Well, since you've told me so much about yourself, I guess it's my turn now." I winked at her, hoping it would clear her mind of the marriage talk. "I grew up in Houston, another big city in Texas several hours from here. My four brothers and I moved to Austin to build this resort. It's been quite the transition." We'd made many transitions in the last couple of years. Not only had we moved, taken on major responsibilities within the resort, but we all become billionaires in the process. "But it's been worth it."

"What did you do before you became a resort mogul?" She sipped her drink, then put it on the bar, giving me all her attention.

"I worked in the hospitality industry, managing a hotel in Houston. That's where I started learning the ropes. My brothers all worked within the same industry, so we each bring something to the table. Some of our cousins came into money—and I mean a lot of money. And we asked them for a loan to build this grand dream we'd come up with."

"Wow." She shook her head. "You all must be such hard workers. I have to admit that I was thinking you probably came from money, and that's how you built this place."

"We did not come from money. Our cousins didn't come from money either. Their grandfather was the breadwinner, and they were his sole heirs. Having got lucky, they wanted to share the wealth with some of their other relatives while helping them get started in businesses. They were looking for good investment ideas, not just handouts. We were their first endeavor, and now that we've done so well, they're helping other family members make their dreams come true too. So while we didn't come from money, we definitely had a lot of help—I don't think a bank loan would've helped us out the way our cousins have."

"They sound like super nice people."

"They are. But they're not just handing out money willy-nilly. They have to believe in the person or people and the product or idea. But yeah, they are good guys." We wouldn't be where we were without the Gentry brothers.

"I think it's amazing that you and your brothers all got into the same sort of work. That you could all agree on how to make this place a success in such a short time is wonderful too—not all siblings have that kind of relationship." She wrinkled her nose a bit as she seemed a little embarrassed. "I feel kind of simple compared to you. I've never dreamed of owning any type of business."

"You're anything but simple. And owning a business isn't for everyone. It's tons of work, and sometimes comes with plenty of headaches." I'd never had so much responsibility in my life. "My responsibility here is to bring in clients from around the world. I had to come up with marketing ideas that could reach the masses in a bunch of different countries. It took hours and hours of research to find out how to market something like this globally. I can't tell you how little sleep I've gotten these past three years."

"Sounds like you could use a vacation yourself, Warner." Her green eyes sparkled as she arched her brows. "Could there be a trip to Ireland in your future?"

"I hear Kenmare is a pretty great place." The idea wasn't half bad. Not that I knew when I could take time off.

"That it is. If you did come for a visit, I would love to be your guide."

"You're making me think about it, I can tell you that." She was making me think about a lot of things. Some that I hadn't thought about in what seemed like a million years.

"You could come and stay at the lodge where I work. It's an amazing place. Nothing like your resort, but great just the same."

"I would love to see it." I meant that, too. "I'll have to try and carve out time in my schedule."

"Is it that tight?" Her lips pulled into the slightest frown.

"I'm afraid it is. The business is still young, so I haven't had more than a day or two off since we began this whole thing. I'm due for some time off—overdue, really. But we don't have anyone right now who can take my place." I did have my assistant, Jezzy. But she'd need more training before I could leave for an extended amount of time. "You've made me think about the lack of free time I have. I need to do something about that." Until she came along, I had no need or desire for time off.

"If your job is bringing in clients from around the world, couldn't you go to other countries to pull in those clients? That would give you a good reason to visit Kenmare." She seemed set on figuring out how to get me to travel to her corner of the world.

And I liked that about her. "For people who've just met, we

sure are looking for ways to spend more time together, aren't we?"

Pink stained her round cheeks. "Let's change the subject, shall we?"

"Nonsense," I joked. "I can't get away for a very long time anyway. It's just an impossibility at this point." Drumming my fingers on the bar, I realized that the fact that I was stuck somewhere—anywhere—bothered me.

Baldwyn traveled around the country for his job. Why couldn't I do the same?

For someone who had such a big issue with commitment to women, it seemed I'd become committed to the resort. So much so that it held me prisoner. Or I held myself prisoner to it.

The resort wasn't holding me, I was holding onto it in some crazy way. I was holding onto my job as if I might lose it, which was impossible, so long as I was an owner.

I need to see a psychiatrist about this fear of loss issue I've got.

"Very well," she said as she picked up her drink. I watched as she lifted the glass to her lips, licking them before touching the glass.

Only when the glass moved up to cover her mouth did I realize how I was staring at her mouth. At that moment, I wanted to kiss those lips more than I wanted anything else. I wanted to taste the drink on them, roll my tongue along hers, and taste every last drop.

Orla wasn't slim or trim. Her shoulders weren't narrow, nor too wide, but just wide enough. She wasn't short either, but neither was she tall. She was the perfect average height. But other than that, there was nothing average about her.

Her dark green dress hung all the way to her ankles, covering her body but not doing anything to hide her curves. Daring, provocative, deadly curves that made my hands itch to run them over every single rounded place of her body.

Earlier, when her group had first come into the lobby, she'd had on a cream-colored sweater with blue jeans and flats. It hadn't done her voluptuous figure justice the way the flowing dress did. The dress hugged her in all the right ways.

Looking all the way down to her shoes, I wasn't surprised to find low heeled pumps. A woman who stood on her feet long hours tending a bar wouldn't wear shoes that might hurt them.

"Did you get enough rest to get rid of the jetlag?" I asked, certain that she'd been suffering that pesky ailment, as anyone would after a long flight.

"I slept all day." She shook her head as her brow furrowed. "I hadn't meant nor wanted to sleep so long. I don't want to waste my time here. I want to make the most of each day, especially since I only have seven nights."

"Stay longer," I said abruptly. For some reason, I didn't want this near-stranger to leave. "I can comp the room for as many nights as you'd like. I mean that. If you teach our bartenders one new cocktail a day, I can make that happen for you." Hell, I could put her on as one of our bartenders, for that matter. But I didn't tell her that, as I knew that was moving way too fast.

A weak smile told me she wouldn't be staying on. "Warner, I only take a week's vacation once a year. I couldn't leave my manager high and dry. It wouldn't be fair to the other staff members if I did something like that without notice. And my parents will surely miss seeing my face in a week's time. I spend Sundays at their house, helping Mum with chores, so she doesn't have to do them by herself. She's getting up there in years and has arthritis, which makes things hard for her."

"You sound as busy as I do." I had to get it through my head that if she and I had anything, it would be short-lived—like, amazingly short-lived. I'd been happy with that at first. Why that was changing all of a sudden mystified me.

This isn't going to work, for neither of us. It just isn't meant to be.

"Well, I'm not busy this week." She took the last sip of her drink, then put the empty glass down. "I'm not about to sit around here either. The resort is lovely, but this is just my nest. I've gotta fly out of it each day before coming back each night and sleeping a bit. Then off to my next adventure in the morning."

"You have an enviable way of looking at life, Orla Quinn."

"Do I?" She shook her head as if she didn't agree. "I look at life for what it is, Warner. We are born, and for a little while, we're stuck to our mother as a means for survival. And then, one day, we can walk, and we don't just walk, we run. We run and run until we drop from exhaustion, then we sleep. And when we wake up, we're running again."

"That's true. I suppose that's true of most babies and little kids." But I'd never looked at things like that, not even once in my life.

"Why do you think we run from the one who has not only protected us but fed us and nurtured us, rocked us to sleep?" she asked me with a serious expression.

I had to think about it for a moment, as I didn't know what she was getting at. And she patiently waited for me to think, which was sort of amazing to me. As the wheels in my head clicked into place, I said, "I suppose we run from our mothers because we inherently seek adventure, and safety is the last place you will find that sort of thing."

A smile lit up her face. "Aye. I like that you thought about that instead of just blowing it off the way many people would. That tells a lot about a person when they take the time to contemplate something."

"I have to admit that this is the first time in a long time that I've done that." Laughing, I couldn't believe how incredible she was. "You're something. Do you know that? You are really something."

"I try to be."

My plan had been to take a page out of my brother's book and play it cool with this woman. And the first ploy had worked like magic. She had come to me. Although it had been indirectly, she'd still come to me. But Orla was genuine and real. And people like that weren't the type you should try to play games with. It was obvious that she would only find the games unattractive and even idiotic. She would think I was a bore, as any Irish lasses would say.

"Alright, I'm gonna come right out and say this to you, Orla Quinn. I like you." It felt good to speak the truth to her. "And I've got more to say."

"Well, can I tell you that I like you too before you give your speech?" Her laughter filled my heart.

I knew getting to know this woman would be worthwhile, if only I gave myself the time to do it. She lived life in a way that I'd never contemplated. This was a rare gift, her coming to my part of the world. I'd be a fool not to accept that gift and give it as much of my attention as possible.

"No speech, I promise. But I would like to be honest with you. I'd like to spend more time with you while you're here. You make me think about things differently. I had no idea I would even like something like that, but I do. I like it very much." Something similar to an electric current sizzled through me as I thought about spending time with her.

Did I want to have sex with her? Well, of course I did. But I wanted more than that. I wanted to get to know her, and I wanted some of her spiritedness to rub off on me. She was that rare of a person—at least, to me, she was.

"I think I would like spending time with you too, Warner." Her eyes glistened as she smiled at me. "So I guess we'll see how much time we get to spend together with that busy schedule of yours."

My schedule was busy; she was right about that. But I could figure things out for a week if I put my mind to it. "I'll deal with that. I'll free up my time."

It felt amazing to have someone who I wanted to be around. And by the way my heart sped up, I knew that it, too, had missed this feeling. I wasn't sure how I would feel when the time for her to leave would come, but at least I was giving it a good try for once.

Maybe this would be a turning point for me where women were concerned. Maybe Orla would open up a door that had been nailed shut for far too long. The main thing was that I now had some hope for a future with love in it. Even if that love couldn't be with the fascinating woman who sat in front of me. At least there was that light at the end of the tunnel, where none had been before.

"I've got something to look forward to now, Warner. Thank you."

"Why don't we start right away? No use in putting things off." We didn't have much time anyway. "I'd like to take you down Sixth Street tonight if you're up for it."

"I'm up for it." She hopped off the barstool. "Let me get my purse from my room, and I'll meet you in the lobby."

"It's a date," I smiled, hoping my heart wouldn't get smashed into pieces by the end of the week.

6

ORLA

When I met Warner in the lobby, he held out his cell phone to me. "Here, put down your cell number in my contacts."

I took his phone and tapped in my number, then handed it back to him. "Okay. If I get lost while we're out, then all I have to do is call you."

"I've got something even better than that." He texted me, and I looked at the message. It said for me to share my location with him. So I did. "Now what?"

"I'll do the same for you." He tapped away on the phone screen then gave me a nod. "We're good to go. This way, if you can't find me, all you've got to do is look at my location. And I can do the same with you. It's very crowded down there, so getting separated can happen pretty easily."

Holding out my hand, I had an even better idea. "Or we can just hold hands so that it doesn't happen at all."

Taking my hand, he grinned and led me out the front door. "Yeah, this will work too."

The valet opened the door of a tall, black truck for me as we approached it. "This is quite the automobile, Warner."

He helped me up. "Step on the running board to make it easier for you to get in."

"Is the height really necessary?" I had to ask, as I had no idea why anyone would want to drive something so high off the ground.

"Necessary?" he asked. "No. But it makes driving way cooler."

After closing my door, he went around and got into the driver's seat. "Like everything else in Texas, we like our trucks bigger than normal ones."

"And you have no issue with driving on the wrong side of the car?" As he took off, I hurried to put on my seatbelt. The road seemed so far below me.

"It's not the wrong side to me." He sped up as we pulled into traffic.

Gasping, I looked at him with wide eyes. "So, you're a speedy driver, then?"

"You've got to use some speed to cut into traffic, Orla." He laughed as he swept around the road, weaving through cars that were much smaller and shorter than his. "Don't tell me you like driving like a grandma."

"I like living through the trip," I informed him. "Driving a bit slower than the other cars has served me well."

"Driving slow in any of America's big cities will get you run off the road. We're rather aggressive drivers here."

"I can see that." Looking up, I found a bar above the door, and instinctively grabbed it.

"You've already found the 'oh shit' bar," he said with a quirky grin.

"The what?" I had no idea if I'd heard him right. "It sounded like you said the 'oh shit' bar."

"Yeah," he said with a nod. "You know, you only grab it when you're thinking, 'oh, shit!' And then, you hold on for dear life."

"I *was* thinking that." I laughed a bit, even though I was terror-stricken.

"Maybe some music will help take your mind off driving." He turned on the radio, and some twangy-sounding man sang about someone leaving him and how whiskey had taken her place. "That's a rather sad song."

"It's in the top ten this week." Taking an exit, he veered off the highway, much to my relief.

But that relief was soon gone as we found tons of cars on this road speeding along too. "My goodness. This city moves fast, doesn't it?"

"Very." He took another turn and then pulled up underneath a bridge, where lots of other cars and trucks were parked. "This is it. We walk from here."

"You can't drive down this street?"

"Not all the way down. Not at night, anyway. They close it off because there're just way too many people walking around from club to club. You'll see. Come on."

Climbing out of the truck was a chore. I didn't want to jump out of it for fear of breaking an ankle. "Um, a little help would be appreciated, Warner."

He came to me, offering his hand. "My lady."

Using his hand to balance myself, I made it down to the ground safely. "You'd hate my car. It's tiny and extremely close to the ground."

"I probably wouldn't even fit." He held my hand as we began walking up the street.

Even though the street was busy with pedestrians, there weren't that many people at this end of the street. Up ahead, I saw tons of lights in many different colors, and the sound of music and people drifted down to us. "It's funny. I'm getting so excited about seeing this."

"People come from all around the world to check out this place. It's like nothing else."

As we got closer, I could smell hints of various foods in the air. "There are cafes down here too?"

"Cafes, boutiques, bars upon bars, tattoo parlors." He squeezed my hand. "We could get matching tats if you'd like."

"My mother would strangle me." His suggestion did make me curious though. "Do you have any tats?"

He put his hand over his right pec. "I've got a broken heart with angel wings."

"Sounds like there's a story behind that."

"One for another time." We came to the end of a block, and we had to stop and wait for the lights to cross. "There are a few bars you've got to see. Maggie Mae's is an Austin staple and Coyote Ugly is a must-see. But if you hear any music that grabs your attention, we can just head into that bar."

As we got to the first block with bars and other businesses, the crowd got a bit thicker. The smells became more intense, and the sounds insane.

Some places had men standing outside as if out of an FBI movie—black suits and sunglasses. "And those men are here because...?" I had to wonder how safe we were if men like those had to be around.

"They're the bouncers. Plus, certain things go on inside certain clubs. If they see someone trying to go inside and think they might not appreciate what's going on in there, they let them know."

"What kinds of things are going on in some of these places?" Now I really felt afraid and knew why Warner had warned my group about this place.

"Well, the saying here is *keep Austin weird*. That's because some weird shit goes on." He pulled me along. "We're not stopping anywhere that might offend you, I can promise you that."

"Thank you." I felt extremely grateful for the man at that moment. "If I were alone, who knows what I might walk into."

Knowing I was perfectly safe, I put all the worry and fear of the unknown behind me and looked around. Neon lights adorned everything along both sides of the street. And as we kept moving, the crowd kept getting thicker and thicker until I understood how easy it would be to lose each other in a place like this.

Different types of music mingled with the sound of people talking, laughing, clapping, and making hooting sounds. We stopped as we came to a crowd of people who were all looking at something we couldn't see yet.

Warner moved us through the crowd until we were at the front of the group. A man squatted near the ground, a can of blue spray paint in his hand. He looked up at me. "Ah, may I paint you, beautiful lady?"

"Me?" I asked with surprise. "I guess so."

"It will only take me a moment." He put the blue can away and grabbed a red one and a brown one. "The hair." The spray paint hissed as he moved both cans in rotating motions over a rather large canvas he'd laid out on the sidewalk.

When he'd finished, my curly hair filled the outer parts of the rectangular board. "That's amazing—it's the exact color of my hair."

Next, he picked up a can of white and a can of tan and made the shape of my face. Then, he picked up a pale green can and made the top part of my dress. Putting the cans away, he picked up a palate and whisked a small paintbrush with such speed that I couldn't tell what color he'd dipped it in until it spread over the face in the painting.

Thin black lines formed my closed eyes, and somehow, he feathered the lines for the eyelashes so well that they looked real. Red lips shaped like a budding rose followed, then golden buttons along the middle of my dress, and he was done. "I present you with this gift. You are a true beauty. Thank you for allowing me to paint you."

Warner was quick to pull out some cash and hand it to him. "I understand the painting is a gift for her. Here's some money for you to babysit the lovely painting for us while I take her on tour. We'll pick it up on our way out."

Nodding, he took the money before propping the painting against the wall behind him. Then, he found another beauty to paint. "How about you, lovely lady? Will you be my next muse?"

Moving along, I held tightly to Warner's hand. "I've never seen anything like that in my life. He was amazing."

"He had you modeling for him, so it was bound to come out well." Tugging me into a bar, he handed the man who stood at the door some money, then in we went. "We need a drink."

"We've barely begun our tour," I said with disappointment.

"We're getting it to go. What will you have?" We stepped up to the long bar, and I saw loads of frozen daiquiri machines swirling about on the wall behind it. "So, we can walk around with these drinks then?"

"Yep. I'm gonna have a beer."

"Me too, then." It seemed like it would be easier to carry around than some fancy cocktail.

With beers in hand, off we went to see more of the sights. It all amazed me. And the people did, too. I saw faces from India, China, Middle Eastern countries. I heard a lot of different languages too.

A hard beat with plenty of electric guitar and bass pulled at me, and I dragged Warner into a club. He came willingly, and we made our way right up to the bandstand where a live rock band was playing. People bobbed their heads and held up their drinks as they sang along with a song I'd never heard before. But I loved the sound.

People kept coming up to stand in front of the stage, and Warner moved behind me, draping his arms around my waist, hugging me from behind, and swaying to the beat. It was surreal to be a part of this scene. I felt as if I were in a movie. And it felt great.

Moving from bar to bar, Warner simply showed me the way and let me take in everything. His presence was unceasing, his interest and amusement palpable. He often smiled as he watched my reactions to everything.

I loved the fact that he wasn't trying to hold my attention. He was letting me enjoy our surroundings without any interference at all. He merely lent me his company, and that wasn't a thing any man had ever done for me before.

Towards the end of the night, we strolled hand in hand along the opposite side of the street. "You love what you do, don't you?" he asked.

"I do."

"I could tell that because you looked over each bar we went to—sometimes extremely thoroughly. And you smiled a lot while you were doing it. What's it like to have a job where you get to interact with so many people on a daily basis?"

"I love people. And I love mixology. It's an art form to me. I can bring together flavors in ways that often tell a story to the drinker's taste buds." I was aware that not many people understood how passionate I was about my job. "My parents think I should use my artistic nature in better ways. But I adore getting to talk to so many people—I don't know that I'd be able to do that if I followed a more traditional artistic career."

"So, you are a real people-person." He chuckled softly. "I'm sort of in the middle. I like to be around people, but I also like my alone time. I didn't have much of that growing up with four brothers. I cherish it now. Maybe too much. It has kept me closed off at times in my life."

"I don't mind being alone. But I like being around people much more. I'm an only child, and I had many lonely times when no one was around, and my parents were too busy to play or talk to me."

"It was rarely quiet in our home. And I never knew when one of my brothers would be in a bad mood and punch me over something for no good reason. I wasn't that way at all. I wasn't about to go up to any of them and punch them—whatever the reason. But they had quick hands and short tempers. It was a relief when they all finally outgrew that crap."

I made a bit of a face at that. "I always had trouble understanding boys growing up. I have lots of boy cousins. But I have lots of girl cousins too, and they're who I hung out with during family parties. Boys have always been a mystery to me. Men, I understand. Boys—you know, in their younger years—I don't know much about them." It seemed to me that I'd missed out on a lot being an only child.

"Most of them are little monsters. Not me, though. I was one of the good ones. Not that it helped me get out of any fights." He changed the way he was holding my hand. Instead of clasping it, he threaded his fingers through mine, which gave me a warm, intimate feeling.

Warner was easy to get along with. That hadn't always been the case with me and men in the past.

Leaning my head against his arm, I wished we had more time. I wished we didn't live so far apart. And most of all, I wished that my heart wouldn't break when I'd have to leave him.

7

WARNER

Although it was three in the morning, I wasn't ready to end the night. "I know this little place that stays open all night where we can get breakfast. They make omelets, waffles, and their breakfast sausage is killer. Are you up for it?"

"I slept all day," she said with laughter laced in her voice. "Of course I'm up for it."

Whisking her away from the party scene on Sixth Street, I made sure to stop back by the artist to grab the painting he'd done of her before we hopped into the truck and headed for Hattie's All Night Café and Dojo. Hattie's son had a passion for karate, and she'd given him some room in the back of the place. It proved to make for an interesting meal whenever they were practicing.

We were seated in a corner booth across from each other in no time, reading their extensive menu. "So, how are you liking your adventure to Austin, Texas so far?"

"You've made it rather amazing." She looked over the menu. "There are so many things to eat here. I'm having a hard time making a decision. I do love that they have pictures on the menu. That's nice."

"I'm going to have the Belgian waffles with breakfast sausage. They bring with it an assortment of syrups—delicious. I like to use a bit of each."

"That does sound good. Do you think they serve sweet tea at this time of the morning?"

I had to laugh. "This is Texas, honey. All places serve sweet tea at all hours of the day and night."

Nodding, she seemed happy with my answer. "I don't know what it is about that stuff, but it's most definitely addicting. I had three glasses with dinner. I never have three glasses of anything."

"Perhaps you should make some kind of a cocktail out of it back home," I offered an idea.

"Oh, heavens no. That would be like giving my patrons crack in a glass. That stuff is way too addictive to pair with any alcohol. But I will want you to help me find what I'll need to make some when I get back home. I think I'll die from withdrawal if I can't ever have it again."

"Lucky for you, it's remarkably simple to make. Some tea bags, sugar, and water, along with ice cubes, and you've got it. If you're feeling adventurous, you could also add some lemon or mint. I'll take you over to my place one day and show you how it's done." I could show her how so many things were done.

Putting the menu down, she propped her elbows on the table, then cupped her face in her hands. "You're the nicest man I've ever met. I mean it. You're not intrusive at all. You give me your attention, but you don't force it on me. I like that."

"I like seeing the world through your eyes." Watching her as she took in all the sights of the night made me appreciate this city all the more.

The waitress came and took our orders, and in moments we had our iced teas in front of us. The way Orla's eyes twinkled as she looked at the frosty glass told me that she was indeed addicted to the nectar-like drink. Lifting the glass to her lips, she took a long sip. "Ah. That's the good stuff right there. I wonder why no one in Ireland has ever thought of this before."

"Who knows, really. My guess is that it has something to do with it being on the cooler side of the world. Naturally, you guys crave warm drinks rather than iced ones."

"I think you might just be right about that." Looking at me, she sat back in the seat. "So, this tattoo of yours. It's been on my mind all night. A broken heart with angel wings, you said. I've been forming possible stories in my mind about why you would have such a thing permanently etched onto your flesh."

Biting my lip for a moment, I wasn't sure if this was the place or time to tell her about my tattoo. So many years had passed since I'd gotten it. But sometimes, I still got choked up when I talked about it.

Moving her hand over the table, she ran her fingers over the back of mine. "It must have a deep meaning for you to be this silent about it. I can feel the pain radiating from you, Warner. Is it a memorial tattoo?"

"Two people that were very important to me passed when I was young." The woman could read me so well. And I was known to be a rather elusive person who wasn't easy to get to know, at least from what other women had told me about myself.

"Your parents," she stated as if she just knew it. "How old were you?"

"Thirteen."

"So young." Slowly, she shook her head. "How unfortunate for you to have lost them right when you'd become a teenager, with all the woes that go along with those years. Not yet a man, no longer a child." Her hand moved over mine, her empathy and compassion almost a physical warmth spreading through me. "How did it happen?"

"A house fire," I whispered, as it was hard to talk through the knot that had formed in my throat. "I was at school. Seventh grade. No one was home but Mom and Dad. The school nurse came and pulled me out of science class. She took me all the way to her office without saying a word."

"You knew something was wrong though, didn't you?" she asked.

"My heart was pounding in my chest so hard that I thought I was going to pass out the entire walk down that long hallway."

"And when she told you?"

"I didn't react for a few minutes. It just didn't seem possible. I just sat there, on that little chair next to her desk, and looked at the floor. As it seeped into my brain, I thought about what I was going to do without them. I wondered if we would be sent to an orphanage. I wondered if they'd been afraid. And that's when I cried. I cried hard and long. I felt like I was losing my mind."

Her hand closed around mine, holding it tightly. "I'm sure your world was torn apart."

"For a while, it was." I stared at her hand, wrapped around mine. I hadn't ever told my story in such detail to anyone. I had told others that my parents had died in a fire, but I never revealed more than that.

"So, what happened after?"

"My oldest brother, Baldwyn, was old enough to take over as our guardian. He was nineteen and worked at a hotel. His boss gave us a place to live in. But it never felt right. To me, it always felt like I didn't have a home anymore. And even though there were five of us living in that house, it felt empty."

"I can imagine that it did." She ran one finger over the back of my hand. "And I'm sure that your heart was shattered."

"It's never really healed," I admitted for the first time to anyone other than myself.

"I doubt it ever will. At least, not entirely. You've suffered one of the most devastating losses anyone can live through. I think that only losing a child could come close to that of your mother or father. And you lost them both at the same time. But you've done well for yourself. It sounds like none of you let it define who you are."

"Somehow, we moved on and up. Don't ask me how because I don't know how any of us did it. I mean, some of my brothers have struggled with some addiction issues. But none so great that they weren't able to overcome them."

"And you?" she asked knowingly. "What did you struggle with, Warner?"

Looking into her eyes, I didn't know if I wanted her to know the truth. But the way she looked into my eyes, with no sign of judgment but only pure compassion, made me confess. "I'm afraid to fall in love."

"Because you're afraid of losing someone you love again?" Nodding, she seemed to understand completely. "It's understandable. But the thing about loss is that it happens to us all. One day, our life ends, and those who loved us lose us. It's part of life. Life is full of many things—love, happiness, promises of a fulfilling future—but also sadness, sorrow, hate, and the horror of losing the ones you love."

"I know all of those things. And I know why I have the issues I do. But knowing hasn't helped me overcome them."

"Time, patience, and forgiving yourself will help." She tapped her finger on top of my hand. "You hold tremendous guilt in your soul, Warner. You've got to let it go. Whatever you think that you did to cause that fire, or whatever was said between you and your mother or father before their deaths, none of that was to blame. It wasn't your fault. And your parents died knowing that you loved them. And they died loving you and your brothers."

My God, how can she know that I felt guilty over having left the house that morning without telling either of my parents that I loved them?

It felt as if my heart was swelling inside my chest. I'd never felt that before. It was odd and sort of uncomfortable. But it also felt as if it was growing, and that could only be good. "You're wise beyond your years, Ms. Quinn."

"I'm a bartender. I've heard enough stories to fill many lifetimes. When you've heard all the things that I have, you begin to find that you've gained this library of knowledge about life and what goes along with it."

"It's a gift." *You're a gift.* "I'm glad you've shared it with me."

"I'm glad that you allowed me to share it with you. You could've held all that inside. I feel privileged that you put your trust in me."

I didn't know who couldn't find trust in her kind eyes and open heart. "You're such a rare gem, Orla Quinn."

Ducking her head, her cheeks went pink as she blushed. "Thank you for the compliment."

Her hand began moving away from mine, and I quickly reached out to stop it, taking it in mine this time, my thumb grazing her knuckles. "No reason for you to be embarrassed, Orla. It's not merely a compliment if it's true."

Looking back at me, she said, "You're the first person who's ever told me something like that. I'm not accustomed to hearing such nice things about myself. Perhaps you bring something out in me that others never have."

"I *know* you bring things out in me that others never have." I liked that about her, too. I liked everything about her. So far.

No one was perfect, of that I was certain. Would Orla's imperfections be minor compared to me?

And what did that even matter, since we couldn't have a real relationship?

The knowledge that whatever this was could only last a week

made my gut swirl. When the food arrived, I tried not to think about Orla leaving. "There's blueberry, strawberry, cinnamon-honey, the standard maple, and lemon syrups. Which will you try first?" I held out the bottle of lemon syrup. "Might I suggest you try this? It's different from anything I've ever tasted before. At least on a waffle."

Taking the bottle away from me, she put a dab onto the edge of the waffle, then cut it off and took a bite. "So tangy." The way she nodded told me that she liked it.

I trailed a long line of blueberry syrup along one side of my waffle. "This is my favorite. I always begin and end with the blueberry."

"I love blueberry scones." She took the bottle and put some of the syrup on the next bite. Her face lit up when she tasted it. "Yum!"

"Maybe I should buy a bottle of this stuff to take home." It might be fun to add some sweetness to the sex I prayed we'd have in the very near future.

"You should definitely buy some."

I doubted she was thinking of the uses I intended it for. But at least she agreed with the purchase. With so little time, I wasn't sure how I'd go about getting her into bed. I wasn't the type to rush things, and I was pretty sure she was the same.

She seemed like the quintessential good girl. And good girls don't often hit the sheets with men they don't know very well. But Orla had gotten insight about me that no one else ever had. I had to hope that would be enough for her to feel safe about sleeping with me.

After breakfast, I took her back to the resort and walked her up to her room. We stood at the door in the hallway. Our clasped hands didn't seem to want to part. "I had the best time I've ever had on a date," I confessed. "I already feel like I know you better than I've ever allowed myself to get to know anyone. And I've pretty much worn my heart on my sleeve with you. You know more about me than almost everyone, except my brothers."

Her brow furrowed as she dipped her head. "I think that's pretty remarkable, Warner."

The way she said it made me think she didn't really believe me. "I find it remarkable, as well. I'm not usually like this with other people—other women."

Lifting her head, she looked into my eyes. "And how am I to know that?"

She had a point. "You'll just have to trust me on this."

"Trust." She nodded. "Yes, it would seem that I will just have to trust you. Well, we shall see what tomorrow brings, Warner Nash. For now, I'm going to climb beneath the sheets and try to get a few hours of sleep. But with how I slept the day away yesterday, who knows when I'll wake up. I know I'm not setting any alarms. This is my vacation, and no alarms are allowed on vacation."

"You know where I'll be." Something felt different between us. The easiness had vanished into thin air. "So just come on down to my office whenever you want."

"Sure." She pulled her hand out of mine, and it had never felt so empty. "Goodnight then. And thank you again for the wonderful night. I truly did enjoy it."

My hands fisted at my sides. I didn't know what to say to make things go back to the way they were. So I did something else that wasn't like me at all.

Taking her by the shoulders, I turned her around to face me, then left a chaste kiss on her cheek. "I had a wonderful time with you too, Orla. Goodnight and have sweet dreams," I whispered directly in her ear. Then I turned and left her standing there.

I felt her gaze on my back and couldn't wipe the smile off my face.

8

ORLA

I opened my eyes to a dimly lit room, the sunlight muted by the thick white drapes but not eclipsed. Lying face up, I looked at the barely moving white ceiling fan overhead. It stirred the air just enough.

Memories of the night before flooded my freshly woken brain. A smile curled my lips as I thought of the kiss on the cheek Warner had left with.

I'd become wary on the ride home. Worried that he would want more from me than I was ready to give. That night had been the best date I'd ever had. But I still didn't know Warner well enough to risk having sex with him.

I wasn't a prude, but I also wasn't into anything too kinky. At my age, I'd heard too many horror stories from friends and patrons about some man wanting to tie a woman up and spank her bottom black and blue after the very first date. Not that I thought Warner was the type to be into that sort of thing, but how was I to know any different?

Plus, I didn't know his reputation yet. And I wasn't sure I would find out that information in time to move on to having sex with him before I had to leave. I wasn't going to rush things —even with the short amount of time we had.

Rolling over, I looked at the clock on the nightstand. *Ten in the morning.*

It wasn't as late as I'd thought it'd be. I wondered if Warner had made it to work yet—not that I was going to dress and rush down to his office. He had work to do. He'd been plain about that. I could entertain myself throughout the day and leave him to his work.

Getting out of bed, I looked at the tablet that lay on the table. *I should book a massage.*

Even though I worked at a resort with a spa in it, I rarely treated myself to one. So I picked up the tablet and made an appointment for an in-room treatment.

After showering, I put on a fluffy white robe and waited for the masseur to arrive and give my body a good pummeling. A knock at the door startled me as I'd just sat down on the end of the bed. "Coming," I called out.

Getting right back up, I opened the door, and there stood a dark-haired woman with a bright smile. "Hello, I'm Alexis Nash, and I'll be your massage therapist today."

Her last name snatched my attention. "Nash? As in the owners of this resort?"

With a nod, she began setting up the portable table. "I'm married to one of the brothers, Patton."

I found that extremely interesting. This woman worked at the resort, and her husband was an owner. "Did you two meet here at the resort?" I had to know. If they had, then it meant that maybe the brothers trolled for women at the resort. And maybe that was what Warner was doing to me.

Only I wasn't here to stay. All there was for me was to become a notch on the man's bedpost. One that might look like wormwood from all the notches he'd taken out of it.

"No, he was my brother's best friend and a friend of our family from way back. He did give me a job though. And our marriage began in an unconventional way, but love won in the end." She pulled out some oils from a black bag and placed them on the small dining table, ready for me to lie down on the massage table. "Are you ready, Miss Quinn?"

I had a little more that I wanted to ask her before she got down to it. "Did you two date before you came to work here?"

"No, we did not." She looked at the table. "Are you feeling anxious about taking off the robe?"

"No." But I did have more questions for her. "So you began seeing each other *after* you came to work here?"

"Not exactly." With her arms folded, she eyed me warily. "Look, I don't know why you're asking me all these questions about my husband, but I will tell you that I don't like it one bit."

I'd irritated her and hadn't meant to do that at all. "I'm sorry. Let me start over. I'm Orla Quinn, and last night I went out with your husband's brother Warner."

The knowing smile told me I didn't have to explain any further. "Oh, I see now. You want to know if he's a mujeriego."

I scrunched my face in confusion. "I'm sorry, a what?"

"A womanizer," she brought me up to speed.

"Yes." She understood me completely. "Is he a ladies' man?"

"No, he isn't at all. And frankly, I'm surprised to hear that he went out with you. He's never gone out with anyone from the resort. Not guests or employees. He's a bit—how to say it? A loner when it comes to women."

"So, he hasn't had loads of girls in his life?" I felt sure a man that good-looking had to have had a harem of lovers.

"He's had two girlfriends in the last three years. And neither lasted even a year." She put her finger to her lips as she seemed to be thinking. "And you know what? I think *he* broke up with them—not the other way around. My husband says Warner is afraid of intimacy—probably from losing his parents at such a young age."

"He told me about what happened to them."

Her jaw dropped. "Are you serious?"

"I am." The wheels turned slowly inside my head. *Maybe he's a good man after all.*

Not that it made much difference. Warner being real with me didn't mean a thing, really. It didn't mean we'd get more time together. It certainly didn't mean we were meant to be together.

He had his life in America, and I had mine in Ireland. Nothing was going to change that. I had a family to keep me rooted in my country, and he had his family and a successful business to tend to in Texas.

Taking off my robe, I got onto the table and let her begin the massage. After draping a sheet over my body, her hands worked my back, loosening the tight muscles. The oils filled my nose with amazing citrusy scents.

"Can I assume from your accent that you're visiting us from Ireland, Orla?"

"You can." Alexis had an accent as well. "And are you from Mexico or Spain?"

"I am from America. Born and raised in Houston, Texas," she said, taking me by surprise.

"America is full of so many different accents that it makes it impossible to know who is from here and who came from another country."

"That is why they call us the melting pot, I suppose." Her hands slid up and down my calves, slicking oil all over them. "Not all people of a Mexican descent have as thick an accent as I do, but I grew up in a neighborhood where most families spoke the language more often than not."

"It's a beautiful accent. Much sexier than mine." I always thought there was something rather seductive about the Latin languages. "I wish I could speak Spanish, but it just won't come out of my mouth correctly."

"My husband tries his best to speak it well, but his Texan accent is just too thick to make the words sound right." Laughing, she ran her oiled hands over my feet.

"Maybe you can help me make a decision, Alexis." I thought I should get some advice from a female before I went and mucked things up for myself. "Warner and I got on well last night. As a matter of fact, we've gotten on well since I first arrived here."

"Sounds romantic."

"It does, rather. But romance isn't really in the cards for me. I mean, not long-term romance. I'm only here for a week. So, I'm asking you what you would do if you found someone very much to your liking but knew it couldn't last longer than a week?"

"That's a hard one, Orla." At least she shared my opinion. "I grew up in a very conservative religious household. Premarital sex was just about the worst thing a woman could consider, but I ended up doing it anyway. I think human nature overrides religious promises at times."

I found that interesting, though maybe not relevant to my current dilemma. "I'm not all that religious—more spiritual, I'd say. But I'm not overly promiscuous, either. I'm not into having sex with lots of men, or men I don't know very well. So this isn't easy for me. I do like Warner immensely. And I can't deny he's gorgeous, and I'm super attracted to him. But I'm not sure if I should act on... whatever it is that we have. Not only do I not want to hurt myself when I have to leave, but I also don't want to hurt him. And I'm not sure I can stop that from happening—there's some kind of connection between us, and I'm pretty sure it will only be harder for both of us when I have to leave if we keep building on that connection."

"You're wondering whether it will be easier to leave if you

don't get too intimate with him." She was a smart woman. "Sure, it might be much easier on both of you if you didn't let things go all the way to sex. But—and this is a strong but—do you think that you and he should just ignore what sounds like an intense connection? How much of a loss would it feel like if you never shared that experience?"

"A big one, I think." Though I was afraid of missing out, I was also afraid of getting lost in our connection. So much so that it had frightened me that if he'd kissed my lips last night, I would've thrown caution to the wind and invited him into my room. "But I wonder if I need to be afraid of that. I mean, I love chocolate cake, but I don't *have* to have it every day. Maybe I will love whatever we do together, but won't need to experience it again."

Coming around in front of me, she worked on my shoulders. "You want my honest opinion, Orla?" I nodded my head, and she continued, "It will most likely hurt you both when you leave, regardless of whether you have sex or not. So why miss out on what could be a great time and something very meaningful just because, in the end, there will be some pain? Pain is inevitable in life."

"Maybe." I still wasn't sure it would be smart to let myself feel so much for a person I could never truly have in my life.

"If you two share these feelings, it's highly likely that you both will somehow manage to get into each other's paths while you're here. Follow your instinct and deal with the aftermath when it arrives." Brushing something soft all over my body, she went on, "A lot of things worth having come with consequences, and this is no different. I mean, think of the consequences of sex —STIs, pregnancy. Pregnancy in itself can be painful or at least uncomfortable. And then there's the actual childbirth and that pain that goes with it—not to mention the post-natal recovery. Yet women still willingly do it."

"That is true. But we go in with our eyes wide open—we all know that we could get pregnant. No contraceptive is one-hundred percent effective. And sometimes, the men who make the babies don't stick around to help you care for them. And yet, most women take that risk for a few moments of pleasure."

"Women sound like fools," she said as she sighed. "Why do we do it, Orla? Why do we do such things?"

"I wish I knew the answer to that. But we do put ourselves through hell, don't we?" I'd put myself in some situations with men before that could've left me in a world of hurt. So, why not have some fun with Warner? He might be able to help me experience some things I never had—and then I could just let the pieces fall where they may?

"Life's just too short to miss certain experiences because of the pain that might come afterwards," she said as she pulled the sheet up to cover me. "And this massage is done. Feel free to put in a review if you'd like. It helps build our reputation when the guests leave good reviews."

"You've helped me in more ways than one. You can expect five stars from me." I sat up on the table, pulling the sheet around to cover myself as I got up. "If my life wasn't so far away, you and I might've ended up sisters-in-law." I had to laugh at how far ahead in the future I was gazing.

Packing up the table, she smiled. "One never knows what the future holds, Orla. I can tell you that from experience. I'd known Patton my entire life and not once had I foreseen our marriage. Never once did I foresee us sharing such passion and such a deep love for one another. Yet, here we are."

"I can see from the love in your eyes when you speak of him that he's a special man. Are all the brothers such good men?"

Nodding, she put the oils back into her bag. "They are all good men. Their lives could've gone very differently after the loss of their parents. Plus, they didn't grow up in money, and yet their newfound wealth hasn't changed any of them a bit. Well, they do dress better than they did before. But personality-wise, they are all the same men."

There was usually a bad seed in any bunch. To think that all the Nash brothers were good made me think it would be even harder to part with Warner at the end of my visit.

But I'm going for it anyway.

9

WARNER

"Heard you were late coming in today," Baldwyn said as he walked into my office, catching me with my feet up on my desk, hands behind my head, gazing at the ceiling, lost in a daydream starring Orla. "And you're not exactly acting like yourself either. What gives?"

Moving my feet off the desk, I sat up straight in my chair then blinked a few times to adjust my vision back to reality instead where it had been—in bed with a beautiful fiery-haired lass. "I had a date last night, that's why I was late today. And I was thinking about it when you came barging into my office uninvited."

"Check your phone," he said as he took the seat across from me. "I've called you like six times."

Pulling my cell out of my pocket, I saw that it had run out of battery. "Well, shit." I plugged it into the charger. "I hope I didn't miss a call from Orla."

"Is that the name of the date?"

"Yeah. Orla Quinn. She's part of the group from Ireland. She's something, bro." My eyes were on the phone, waiting for the moment when it would have enough charge so I could turn it on and see if I had missed her call or text. "Maybe this is why she hasn't come to see me yet." It was a little after noon, and I'd been wondering if she was sleeping in. But now I knew she might think I was ignoring her, and that wasn't going to work for me.

"You went out with one of our guests?" Baldwyn asked with shock in his voice. "You've never done that before."

"There's something about her—I couldn't pass up the chance to ask her out. And we had the best time, too. She's got this way about her that makes it easy for me to be with her—whether we're deep in conversation or not." I couldn't explain it, but she had drawn me in from the start, and I didn't want to find my way out. "From the moment I saw her, I just couldn't take my eyes off her."

"I'm glad you followed your gut and asked her out. It's been a long time since you've shown an interest in anyone." One brow cocked as he looked at me with the oddest expression. "But you said she's from Ireland. And that's not so good, is it?"

"There're other ways to look at that." I'd wrestled with that from the get-go. "There won't be an ugly breakup. And that's always a good thing."

"There also won't be a lasting relationship," he said. "And that's a bad thing. Do you think you've subconsciously chosen her because she's not attainable for the long haul?"

"Who knows?" I certainly had no idea why I was so drawn to her. "She's gorgeous. Probably that's why I singled her out of the crowd."

"Lots and lots of gorgeous ladies come through our doors, Warner. I don't think that's the only reason." Tapping his chin with his forefinger, he seemed set on figuring out the inner workings of my mind. "This is a step in the right direction though. At least you're going out with someone, and you seem to be enjoying it. You did say that you feel like you can talk to her. So, have you told her about our parents?"

"I have."

His jaw hit the floor. "You don't tell people about that."

"I know."

"This is really bad, Warner."

"I can't think of it that way." There was no point. "I have to think that even though our time together will be short, I will enjoy it and her. And I'll let myself experience that for a week. Who knows? I might come out of this thing with some healed wounds. Wounds I've been carrying around for too long."

"Warner, what if all this does is deeper than those wounds? It might just make you even more convinced you'll always lose the people you love. I don't want this to backfire and give you an even harder with falling in love," he sounded so sure that I was doomed.

But he wasn't in my head, and he couldn't see the future, so he couldn't possibly be sure about anything. "Look, I know this sounds far from ideal. But I've never been into self-sabotage before."

That dark brow of his cocked at me again. "Oh yeah? Then what do you think it is when you start seeing a woman then abruptly end the relationship for no good reason?"

I thought that I'd been doing a favor to the women I'd let go. "At least I never let them invest too much time in me before letting them go. At least I don't tell lies and make promises that I can't keep. And the great thing about seeing Orla is that both of us know this will have to end. We even know what day it will end. We're adults. We can make our own decisions. If she's not worried about this, then why should I be?"

"Maybe she *is* worried about getting hurt and hurting you. Maybe that's why you haven't heard from her yet."

I didn't like to think that way. "I'm sure she's just sleeping in. She told me that she had slept all day yesterday. Maybe the travel left its toll on her. I'm sure that's what it is." I held out my phone to show him that I had no missed calls or messages from her. "See, she hasn't tried to contact me yet. She's asleep, is all."

"And if she's not?" he asked with narrowed eyes. "Then will you leave her alone and stop doing this to yourself and her? I mean, you came on to her, right? It wasn't the other way around, I'm sure."

"How are you so damn sure that she wasn't the one who came on to me?" I thought that was a pretty rude assumption—I wasn't that bad of a catch.

"You said that from the moment *you* saw her, *you* couldn't take your eyes off her."

"And what's so wrong about that? People do that all the time. People have flings—especially while on vacation." I knew what I said was true, but a part of me wondered if I was trying to convince myself of it as much as I was trying to convince my brother.

"Yeah, some people do—but not you." He met my eyes, making sure his words sank in. And they did. But I still wasn't willing to forget about Orla. "And maybe she's rethinking spending a whirlwind week with you."

"Baldwyn, I know you're just trying to look out for me, but we know this will end. I don't think we'll fall in love knowing that we only have six more nights together." And I hoped we'd soon be spending the whole of the nights that way too.

His lips formed into a thin line as he came up with his next argument. "You're right, I am worried about you. Mom and Dad's death messed with your head, Warner. How couldn't it have? You were so young—we all were. And you've yet to see someone about that, even though it's already affected every relationship you've had. Forgive me if I don't see how this one is going to be different—that this is just one more in a long line of unhealthy relationships."

"It does feel different though. I'm going into this with eyes wide open. It's not like I planned this anyway, it just happened. We met, sparks flew—end of story."

"Here' how I think it will go. You met, sparks flew—hearts got broken."

I was used to living with a broken heart. "I'll be fine."

"Sure you will," he said sarcastically. "You weren't fine to begin with."

"But I was." I had my hang-ups, but I was perfectly okay. "I'm not some broken man, Baldwyn. I can handle my business just fine."

"You can handle your business more than fine. It's your love life that you can't handle. Do you have any idea how many of your ex-girlfriends have come to me or one of your other brothers to ask what they did wrong to make you dump them?"

"I had no idea that any of them had done that." I didn't think that was appropriate of them, nor did I like that my brothers didn't tell me about it. "And why haven't any of you mentioned this?"

"Because we all know why you did it, and we always tell them that it wasn't anything they did," he let me know. "Would you really have taken it well if any of us had told you?"

"No." I wasn't taking it well now. "You know, some of them did do things that turned me off. It wasn't always just me. But I did always take the blame for the way things ended. I wasn't a complete jerk about it."

"I know that you never entered any relationship with evil intentions. But you also never went into one with an open heart."

"How am I supposed to go into one with an open heart when you've pointed out that the one I have is broken?" He was starting to get on my nerves in the way only a brother could. I'd had just about enough of this conversation. "If you're worried that I'm going to get my heart broken, then rest assured that I'm looking at this with the same heart I always have—the one you've so kindly pointed out doesn't work properly."

Baldwyn sighed, rubbing his hands down his face. "Look, maybe that's the thing I'm really worried about here—that it seems like you finally are going in with an open heart. It's obvious you genuinely clicked with this chick." He sighed heavily again. "I can see it in your eyes. There's something there that I've never seen in them before—and I don't want this to blow up in your face."

I'd seen it in my eyes too. "I think knowing that this will end without a fight helps take the pressure off."

"You know, just because something ends without a fight doesn't make it hurt any less." With a nod, he got up, signaling the end of our argument. "I'm going to walk away to give you time to reach your own conclusion. I only hope that you've heard at least some of what I've said."

"I'll think about what you've said." Even if I didn't agree with him.

"Good." A smile curled his lips. "That's all I ask."

As he left my office, I got up to stretch my legs as I'd been sitting too long. I had to get out of my office for a while. Orla had my number if she woke up and wanted to see me.

Walking down the hallway, I decided I should grab a quick bite. Something small, as I wanted to take Orla out to dinner later. Even if my oldest brother disapproved, I wasn't going to stop seeing her.

I'd never felt more strongly about anything where a woman was concerned. I wasn't going to take the safe path and miss out on what seemed very special to me. And I hoped Orla felt the same way.

But there was a thread of doubt about that. She'd gotten so distant on the drive back to the resort last night. And the whole vibe at the door to her room was on the cooler side. But I knew she hadn't expected me to kiss her on the cheek and not ask for more. I hoped that would show that she was special to me. Even though it couldn't last, it wasn't something I wanted to rush either. I just hoped she was willing to give it a chance.

Rounding the corner to the café, I found Orla walking towards me with a bagel in hand. She froze in place, her green eyes wide.

I kept going, walking right up to her even though I wasn't sure what that look was all about. "I thought you were still sleeping."

"I've been up for a while. I got a massage. And then I got a mani-pedi." She wiggled her polished fingernails. "I honestly didn't expect you to be available during the day. I didn't want to bother you."

"I don't consider you a bother at all." Taking her hand, I looked at the color of her nails. "Nice. I love shiny red nails."

"I usually go with a more neutral shade like soft pink or champagne. But I thought that since I'm in the very colorful U.S.A., I would be more daring."

Seeing her nails had stirred a memory inside of me. And for once, the memory didn't leave me reeling with pain. It left me feeling warm and happy. "My mother also liked to paint her nails red. And they were short like yours. I love the way they look."

"Wow." Blinking a few times, she added, "This is the first time I've ever gotten them red. I just saw the color and told the manicurist that I wanted it. I had no idea that it would stir you."

"I have to admit that, most of the time, when I'm reminded of either of my parents, I tend to withdraw—from both the memory and whatever reminded me of it. But I don't feel like withdrawing from you at all. I actually feel like hanging onto you. How about we get some lunch?"

She held up the half-eaten bagel. "I'm not hungry."

It was just a bagel. I didn't think that that alone could possibly fill her up. Her answer made me wonder if my brother was on to something when he'd said maybe she'd decided not to spend as much time with me as I wanted.

But I was still going to try. "Even though it's on the chilly side today, we could take a walk in Zilker Park. It's really pretty. You've got to see it. And later, we can go to eat somewhere nice." My heart raced as I waited for her answer. If she came up with another reason not to go, then I knew she'd had a change of heart.

"Warner, I understand that you're busy. You were extremely clear about that last night. I don't want to get in the way of your work."

I didn't like her answer. "Are you just making up excuses not to hang out with me?"

"Heavens no!" Absolute shock filled her pretty face as she shook her head. "I just don't want you to think that you've got to spend a lot of time with me, is all. I *want* to hang out with you. But I don't want to get in your way."

"*You* are *not* in my way. Even if you were, I would make time for you, Orla. So come with me to this amazing park, then we'll go have something delicious for dinner?" I crossed my fingers behind my back.

"If you're sure that I'm not keeping you from pressing work, then I would love to go with you."

Thank God.

10

ORLA

"Can we have a real conversation before we go anywhere? You know, in private." I had learned a lot about him from what his sister-in-law had told me, and I had to be sure that we were on the same page here. He'd been through so much already. I didn't want to cause him any further pain—even if pain was a part of life.

"Come on." He took my hand, pulling me with him. "We can talk in my office."

As soon as we stepped into the lobby, Mona and her mother caught sight of us. Mona waved, and then her eyes darted to our clasped hands. She dropped her hand unceremoniously and turned away.

Good. I don't want to talk to her anyway.

Warner led me to his office, closing the door behind us. "Have a seat on the sofa, and we'll talk about whatever you want, Orla." He sat down beside me but left some space between us.

"I talked to Alexis this morning. She was the one who gave me the massage."

His jaw tightened as he nodded. "I see."

"She didn't say anything bad about you, so don't worry about that. But she did tell me that you've never dated any of the guests or employees from the resort. And she also told me that you've had relationships that didn't last long and that *you* ended them."

"She's right."

I took his hand. "Warner, I'm afraid that I might hurt you if we keep going the way we are. I'm afraid that when the time comes for me to leave, it might do more damage to your heart than has already been done. And I don't want to be a part of that."

"And what about *your* heart, Orla?" he asked with sincerity in his blue eyes. "Doesn't your heart matter?"

"It does matter. But mine hasn't been smashed to pieces the way yours has. So mine is on the back burner for now. I don't want to sound presumptuous, but I know there's something special between us, and I don't want to see you hurt."

Moving his hand to caress my cheek, he looked deeply into my eyes. "Orla Quinn, you are truly one of the best people I've ever had the pleasure of knowing."

I laughed at that. "You still hardly know me, Warner. But I do care about you, and I don't want to cause any further damage."

"Honestly, you've already done much more good than you could ever do harm. There's something therapeutic about talking to you, spending time with you. I think you're just what the doctor prescribed."

"But what about when I'm not here anymore? Will you still feel that way?"

"You'll leave your mark on me, that's for sure." He chuckled. "You and I keep getting bogged down in what will happen when you have to leave. Let's make a pact to stop talking about that. It *will* happen, and we both are fully aware of it."

"And you'll be happy with only the memories we make?" I knew I would be, but I wasn't sure about him.

"I *will* be happy with just those. And I'll be happy making those memories too." His thumb grazed my lower lip, heating me up inside. "And I think that knowing that I can share myself with someone will help me grow a little."

"So, you're using me as therapy?" I laughed. "I can deal with that."

"Good. Because I'm ready to get moving with us. We only have six nights, after all. No time to waste. And on the morning that you leave, we will part on good terms. I think it's what I love the most. No breaking up. No tearful goodbyes."

"What makes you so sure you won't cry like a baby?" I laughed again. "I'm not a thousand percent sure that I won't."

"If you feel like crying, then do it. Hopefully, they'll be tears of joy from what we meant to each other while you were here."

It sounded to me like he'd been thinking things through and wasn't merely shooting from the hip. As long as he was aware of the reality of things, I was okay with moving forward. "So I'm going to go change into something that I can take a stroll in without making my feet sore." I'd worn low heels with a long skirt, and that wouldn't do for what he had in mind.

"I'll be right here when you're ready. I'll see about making reservations for us somewhere really nice. What's your favorite type of food?"

"I like seafood." Getting up to go to my room, I left him making plans.

As the elevator doors opened on my floor, I saw Mona standing there. She looked at me with her beady eyes. "And what do you think you're doing with Warner Nash, Orla?"

Stepping off the elevator, I huffed. "Why do you care? And I just saw you down in the lobby. What has you back up here?"

"Mum left her purse in the room and asked me to come and

fetch it for her. And what do you mean, why do I care? We *are* travel mates. We're supposed to look out for one another. And I'm worried about you. It looks as if you and Warner are a thing."

"A temporary one," I let her know. Mostly so she'd stop flirting with him.

"He's very handsome. Aren't you afraid it'll be hard when you have to leave?"

"He and I have discussed that, and we're both happy to only spend the week together. With that said, you probably won't be seeing much of me, it seems."

"Have you told your mum and pop about what you're doing?" she asked.

"I have not, and I don't intend to tell them either. They don't need to know everything about my love life. It would be nice of you to keep this to yourself." I knew she couldn't keep her mouth shut. But I had to try.

"Mum won't be mute on this. You can be sure of that. She saw you two holding hands as well. For all I know, she might be on a call with your mother as we speak."

There were pros and cons to living in a small town—and traveling with your neighbors. This was unmistakably a con. Someone would surely tell my parents about Warner, and that was a headache I didn't need. "I'll call her myself. Let your mother know that." If anyone was going to deliver this news, it would be me.

Leaving her, I went to the room and began pulling off my clothes as I dialed Mum, putting the phone on speaker so I could change while talking to her. "Orla? Is that you, dear?"

"It is me, Mum. I'm calling to let you know what I'll be doing while I'm here in Texas." I grabbed a thin sweater in case the temperature dropped. The Texas winter weather was nothing compared to the cold of Ireland's winter season, but better safe than sorry.

"And what is it that you will be doing?" she asked with no concern in her voice.

I thought that was a good sign that she wasn't worrying about me. "One of the resort's owners and I hit it off yesterday. He's going to take me to see the sights this week, so I'll be going about with him some. I just wanted you to be aware of that. You know how nosy some of the people in this group are—I just wanted you to hear it from me first."

"Ah, yes. I'm glad you called to tell me. Some people love to stir the pot. I trust your judgment, and I'm sure this man will keep you safe while you're away. That's what matters the most."

"Yes, he will keep me safe." And I hoped he'd keep me warm as well. "How's Pop's back doing?"

"Awful. He's laid up in his easy chair, watching horrid comedies and laughing, then moaning when his laughter is causing his back to spasm. I told him to watch something that doesn't make him laugh so much, but he told me he wants to be cheered up."

"Silly man." With things all taken care of with my parents, I felt much better. "Well, I'm about to head out to a park with Warner now, and then we'll get something to eat for dinner."

"Have fun, dear. Bye now."

"Bye." I gave myself a thorough look over in the full-length mirror. Jeans, a light sweater, and sneakers would work for the park. But I knew they wouldn't work for dinner if Warner was trying to go all out—and based on our conversation earlier, I knew he would be planning something special. "This is impossible."

Looking through my clothes, I couldn't find anything that would work for both occasions. With a shrug, I knew he'd have to bring me back here to change clothes before we set off for the restaurant.

I was a different person with Warner than I was in any of my past relationships. It was easy to be open with him. Everything was just so easy.

If I learned anything from Warner, I wanted to learn how to have experiences that would somehow shape me. I'd never looked at my previous relationships as opportunities to grow. There wasn't one instance I could recall where I felt that I'd either learned something about myself or the person I was with.

It hadn't occurred to me that I hadn't really been open with any man in my past. I'd been relatively closed off, keeping my opinions to myself. And I didn't argue with any of the men I'd seen either. My motto was *you do you*. But now that I thought about it, that attitude seemed pretty insensitive and shallow.

It made me realize that I'd been an uncaring partner in all of my romantic relationships—worrying more about myself than the relationship. I was a much better friend than a lover, it seemed.

Perhaps my attitude resulted from being an only child. I'd never had to focus on anyone in my life. And I'd never had to share my parents' attention either. The one thing I knew for sure was that I had to practice doing the things I hadn't ever had to do. At least, I would have to if I ever wanted to have a long-lasting and happy relationship.

Looking at Warner's issues had made me want to discover some of my own. So far, the temporary relationship we were on the verge of having had already opened my eyes to my own faults. Which I found to be a good thing.

A person can't grow if they think they're perfect. We all have imperfections that could use some working on. I was just glad that it had finally come to my attention.

Just as I stepped off the elevator in the lobby, I saw Warner coming out of his office with a slight frown. Going up to him, I had to ask, "What's with the frown?"

"The place I wanted to take you to has been closed down due to some health code violations."

"We can go somewhere else. It doesn't have to be fancy, Warner. Anywhere will be fine." I looped my arm through his as we headed for the door. "Less fancy would actually be even better. It'll mean that I don't have to come back here to change clothes before we eat."

"I hadn't thought about that." He looked at his suit, then nodded. "I'll have to stop at my place to change too. I can't possibly walk around the park in this."

"Good. It'll be nice to see you in something other than a suit." He looked damned good in a suit. But I was curious what he looked like in something much less formal.

I supposed any man looked good in an expensive suit. I did bet that Warner would look nice in anything, though. And he'd look especially good without anything on. I was sure of it.

What I wasn't sure was how long I should wait before having sex with him. He made things tingle inside of me without any effort. I was sure the sex would be off the charts amazing.

I'd never had fantastic sex. I'd had the kind of sex that got the job done—most of the time—and that was about it. It would be nice to know what amazing sex felt like. Even if I never had it again, it would be nice to know it did exist.

Up until meeting Warner, I'd thought people had to be exaggerating about sex being so amazing. Then again, I usually only heard such things from people who had met *the one*—their words, not mine.

Maybe that was the real difference between a good relationship and a bad one—the sex. It would make sense then that a man or woman would want to lock down their partner if they ever found that kind of explosive connection.

If that was so, then how would I handle leaving him? *And here I go again, thinking about when I leave. I've got to stop doing that.*

"Do you like to sing, Orla?" Warner asked me as he helped me climb up into his tall truck.

"Um, like in front of people?" I wasn't that brave.

"No, like *with* them."

I had no clue what he was talking about. "I can carry a tune, but that's about it."

"That's all you'd have to do." He closed the door, then walked around the truck.

I watched him. His broad shoulders moved like those of a panther. Effortless. Perfect posture, hair, skin, and when he caught me looking at him, his smile was perfect as well.

Getting into the truck, he chuckled. "Checking me out, huh?"

"I thought I'd get a good look at you before you put our lives in danger with your speedy driving—just in case it's the last nice thing I see." I grabbed the *oh shit* bar and held on. "I'm ready."

Laughing, he gunned the engine, then sped away, leaving me breathless. Only this time, I was breathless with excitement to be sitting next to the man beside me.

11

WARNER

"We're out of traffic. You can let go of that bar now, Orla."

Her knuckles had turned white as she was clinging to the bar. "I think it's glued to it now." She pried her fingers loose, then put her hands in her lap, still a bit anxious about my driving.

The neighborhood I lived in was on the outskirts of the city, where there was much less noise to deal with and less traffic too. "We'll be at my place soon. You won't have to endure much more driving. At least for a little while."

"Maybe I'll get used to it."

"If I take you lots of places, you just might." I thought that sounded like a brilliant idea. But being that the state of Texas is so big, that would definitely mean some overnight trips. And we hadn't gotten to the point where of spending our nights together.

Pulling through the elaborate entrance to the subdivision I lived in, I saw her eyes widen as she took it in. It was a bit over the top. Waterfalls on each side that made small streams that ran over rocky beds. Even though it was winter, the greenery the community developers had chosen stayed green all year round.

"This is nice, Warner." Her eyes scanned the lavish grounds the gorgeous homes were built on. "I should've known a man with your wherewithal would live in such a stately place."

"You mean money?" I had to chuckle. "Yeah, it made no sense to live in a shack when I have the bucks to afford a bit more than that."

Cruising at a slow speed through the winding streets, I pulled up to my driveway, pushing the button on my visor to open the gate. "A gated entry? Fancy."

"Most of the homes have them. It's common here." I parked in front of the house and watched her as she looked at it.

"Two stories?" She turned to me. "You must share this place with someone."

"Nope." I got out of the truck and went around to help her out. "Come on, Orla."

She took my hand and hopped down. "You live in this huge place alone?"

"All alone."

"Oh, but you must have servants." She nodded as if sure about that.

"I have a maid service that comes in twice a week and a gardener who takes care of the lawn whenever it needs it. No one lives with me." Keying in the code, I opened the door, and in we went.

The entryway was meant to leave an impression, and it was the first thing Orla noticed. "The ceiling goes all the way up to the second story. I love light fixture—minimalistic, but that gold rope and silver orb only highlight the grandeur."

"My brother, Patton, designed the interior. He knows my tastes, and so, this house really suits me." Taking her hand, I tugged her along. "If you think the foyer is nice, wait till you see the main living area."

Although I hadn't entertained a crowd yet, the sprawling living room looked as if it could easily hold twenty to thirty people without anyone feeling crowded. My favorite part of the living area was the fireplace.

"My goodness, that fireplace is spectacular. It's a two-sided one, isn't it?"

"That's the main dining room you see on the other side of it. This is a house made for entertaining. I'm not sure why I wanted it so badly, since I've never entertained in it yet. But I love the place." Tugging her along, I wanted to show her where I really hung out. "Come with me."

Walking through the barely used kitchen, I had to pull her along, as she wanted to check out every little detail of the gourmet kitchen. "This kitchen rivals the one in the restaurant at the lodge I work at. Are you a chef as well?"

"No. But I can grill like nobody's business." I would have to make her some of my barbeque before she left.

Taking her out the kitchen door, I showed her the outdoor kitchen. She ran her hand over the stainless steel barbeque pit that was tucked into an island of natural rock. "You grill on this?"

"I do." Holding out my arm to gesture to the entire patio, I went on, "This is where I spend a lot of my time when I'm home. I love it out here."

"I can see why." She looked at the trees in the yard. "I'm glad to see that the people who built these homes didn't cut down the trees. What kind are those?"

"Oak trees." I had three of them that shaded the entire yard. But there was more to show her. "Come on, let's head inside."

Pulling her along, she seemed to want to linger a bit. "This is an amazing place you call home, Warner."

"I think so too. I'm very proud of it." I took her to the den, where I spent the majority of my time. A large television hung on one wall and two recliners sat in front of it. "This is where I hang out the most when I'm not outside."

"So, you watch a lot of television then?" she asked, as that was the main item in the room.

"Not a lot of it. Mostly, I work. But I come in here to watch television most nights before bed, to help me wind down." Grabbing the remote, I turned the TV on, then handed it to her. "Here you go. Watch something to entertain yourself while I go change clothes."

"Okay." She took the remote from me, our fingers barely touching. Our eyes met. Her lips parted a bit as if she were about to say something. But then she just sighed and took it from me. "Thank you."

Gulping, I found my hand shaking and shoved it into my pocket. "I'll be right back."

Hurrying away, I wondered why I had such strong reactions to her. With even the tiniest of touches, I found myself craving her luscious lips with an intensity that nearly turned me into some savage.

Flashes of ideas flooded my head as I walked away from her. Ideas about how I could take her by the hair, yank her head back and kiss her like no one had ever kissed her before. Images came too, and I felt my heart pounding as I went into my bedroom, closing the door behind me. I felt like some giddy teenage boy who couldn't tell his ass from a hole in the ground.

I need a cold shower.

Twenty minutes later, I'd showered, calmed down, and dressed for a walk in the park. Joining her again, I found her reclined in my favorite chair, watching a documentary on the Philippines' indigenous people.

She looked at me as she pushed the button to bring the

recliner back to its original position and asked, "Did you know that Filipinos are not the first people to inhabit the Philippines?"

"I did not know that." I offered her my hand to help her up after she clicked off the television.

"The first people there were the Austronesians, and they're still there to this day." Her hand curled around mine as she and I headed for the front door. "My question is, if they called the people who were there originally Austronesians, then why not call the place they live in something like Austronesia, instead of the Philippines?"

"Perhaps it comes down to history, like it did in America. You know, the native people who lived here were called Indians. Which couldn't be more inappropriate, as this land was not India as Christopher Columbus had thought it was." Closing the door behind us, I took her to the truck.

But when I went to help her up, she just shook her head and reached inside, grabbed the bar above the door, and pulled herself up. "I've figured it out, Warner."

"You sure have." Closing the door, I couldn't wipe the smile off my face, even if I'd tried. I admired women who liked to do things for themselves instead of waiting for someone else to do it. I didn't need a woman to pretend to be too weak, petite, or feminine.

As soon as I got into the truck, she asked, "How do the Indians—I mean, the Native Americans—feel about things here in America now?"

"That's a hard question, Orla." I wasn't knowledgeable about that at all. "That's not my forte. The only thing I know for sure is that the government has given them some pieces of land, that they call reservations, to live on."

Her jaw dropped. "And they can't leave those places?"

. . .

"No, no, it's not like that." I had no idea what she knew about America. "Of course they can leave the reservations. They can live wherever they want. But again, I don't know much about it."

"It's your own country, and you know so little about these people?" Her raised brows told me she wasn't impressed.

"They don't teach us a lot about that in our schools."

"And why not? It's *your* unique history and no one else's. Don't you want to know about the people who lived on this land long before you did?"

"If I say not really, are you going to punch me in the arm?" I had a feeling that she might.

"I don't think I'll resort to violence over it, no." Laughing, she lightened up a bit. "It's just odd to me that it's not taught in schools."

"Well, our history doesn't exactly make us look good. We did take their land away from them and commit genocide against them. And I think there are plenty of unresolved issues between many of the existing tribes and the government. Maybe it's because we might come off as the bad guys that we're not taught about them in school." That's about all I could come up with. "You know, like who wants to find out that our country was created in such an immoral and even evil way?"

"But aren't most nations formed that way?" she asked with one raised brow. "Wars have ravaged the entire world since the beginning of mankind."

The woman was smart, I had to give her that. "Perhaps you were taught to embrace that knowledge because you come from such an old world with tons of history. This country is relatively new in comparison."

As we pulled into the park's parking lot, I couldn't help but notice that she hadn't even grabbed the *oh shit* bar once on the way over. "Hey, we made it without you breaking out into a sweat."

"I guess I'm getting used to your driving." She opened the door and hopped out of the truck.

Meeting her in front of it, I draped my arm around her shoulders while she scanned the scene before her. "That's the Colorado river you're looking at. We'll walk over to Barton Creek, where Barton Springs feeds the water source. The water is so clear that you can see right through it."

Moving her head to take in the whole scene, she whispered, "This place is amazing. You have to show me everything."

Slipping my arm off her shoulders, I took her hand, and off we went. "It looks like we'll be here until dark if you want to see it all."

"I do want to see it all. This is what I came for, Warner. I love nature, and even though this is in the middle of a big city, it is still natural."

As we walked, I thought it was the perfect time to get to know her better. "So, you live alone, right?"

"I do live alone. Remember, I told you about my grandparent's home that I inherited?"

"I do." I hadn't said that right at all. "Have you ever lived with anyone? I mean other than your parents."

"No." She pointed to something that scampered up a tree as we approached it. "What's that?"

The bushy tail disappeared in a hole on the tree trunk. "A squirrel."

"That was a squirrel? But it was so fat."

"They get plenty to eat, I'm sure." I still hadn't gotten the information I was after. "Being that you're in your late twenties, I'm guessing that you've had some serious relationships."

"I've had a handful of relationships in my life. A few of them were rather short, lasting only a year or so. And then I had one that lasted only a few months. There's one that's been on-again, off-again since high school. But it's mostly been off."

"And why is that do you think?"

"I think that's because he's not the right man for me. If he were, then surely we would've figured things out by now, right?"

"I agree." Although I knew I wasn't going to be a part of her future, I couldn't help but feel slightly relieved that she hadn't found someone who'd taken her heart yet.

How selfish of me. But that was the truth.

12

ORLA

As Warner and I got closer to Barton Creek, we heard the trickling sounds echoing off the canyon wall. Laughter mixed in with the sound, telling me unseen children were playing in the waters.

His hand securely held mine as we went down a pathway through somewhat thick trees. "Watch your step. It gets rocky up here near the water. I don't want you to slip and fall into the water."

"Perhaps we should slow down a bit, so that doesn't happen. There is a slight chill in the air, and getting wet might give me a cold. The last thing I want is to be sick."

He slowed his pace. "Yeah, good idea."

As we eased through the trees, they suddenly opened up, and there it was—the crystal clear water. "This is beautiful!"

Looking up the creek, I saw some children splashing around in a shallow area. Their mother was looking at her cell phone as they laughed and played in what had to be frigid water.

"Come on, there are some falls ahead that you've got to see." Warner tugged me along, being careful where he stepped. "Step on the same rocks as me."

Following him, I tried to look at everything as we moved along the shoreline. But I had to watch where I stepped, so I knew I was missing things. "I can't believe this is right in the heart of this city."

"It's a hidden gem alright." He kept going.

And I kept listening to the sounds. "I hear the waterfall. But it doesn't sound that big to me."

"It's a small one. But it's still pretty. Way up the creek, not in this park though, there are more spectacular waterfalls. We could take a road trip so you can see them if you'd like. Of course, that would have on some other day."

"I would love to do that." We stopped, and I could finally look up. A series of large rocks rose in the creek, making for a three-foot waterfall that moved through the rocks, carving them into craggy shapes. "Oh, this is beautiful."

"I thought you'd like it." He pulled me up to stand beside him, running his arm around my waist and pulling me closer. "It's got a lot of detail if you really look."

"I see. The clear water has made an impact on the rocks, hasn't it?" Thousands, maybe even millions of years, had marked the area. "Ancient."

"Yeah. I suppose it is." His lips pressed against the top of my head. "Thanks for coming here with me. I see it very differently through your eyes."

"Can you imagine the native people who must've lived around here? Can you believe what a utopia they lived in? I'd fight to the end not to be kicked off this land." It was hard for me to believe that people could've been moved away from this paradise.

"They may have met their ends trying to stay here," Warner whispered as if giving reverence to spirits that might still be lurking nearby. "Odd that I've never thought about that until now."

"I agree." I ran my arm around him, giving him a little side hug. "This *is* your part of the world, Warner. You should know all there is to know about it."

"I've been busy." He chuckled. "Not that it's a good excuse for being ignorant of my homeland."

"That seems to be pretty common with most Americans. The mother of those children back there was so busy with her cell that she didn't see the expressions of pure joy on her children's faces. Sad. Where I'm from, people are more important than anything else."

Nodding, Warner seemed to agree with me. "I have to admit that most of us do have a tendency to ignore what's right in front of our faces. Technology and work have taken places as top priorities."

"It's never too late to change, Warner." Inhaling the cool air, I tried to slow myself down. I didn't want to appear as if I was judging Warner or his country. "But as you said, technology takes priority. Maybe that's only because it's relatively new and always evolving. Perhaps that's why it's so addictive. I'm sure, with time, things will settle into place. At least where technology is concerned."

"Work is another story, huh?" Warner asked with a chuckle. "The almighty dollar makes slaves of many of us—myself included."

"You don't have to let it, do you?" I ran my thumb along his knuckles as I smiled at him.

"Our resort is in its first phases. I'm afraid that work will have to come before most things for a while longer. We don't want to sit back now when we've got a good head start."

"Spoken like a true businessman. I suppose that's why I'm just a barmaid. I put my life first. I always have and always will. I can't imagine any job changing that." We'd walked around the park for so long that the sun was beginning to set. "Perhaps we should start heading back to your car. It's going to be dark soon."

Turning back from the way we'd come, he led me along the creek. "You seemed to have had a good time walking around here today. I'll have to show you as many of my state's natural areas as I can in the coming days."

"That sounds good to me." But I wasn't sure he'd actually have the time to do that. "If your work will allow it."

"I'm going to make sure I have time. You're only going to be here five more days. I'm sure I can take some time off. I haven't taken any thus far. I've earned it."

I liked that I'd rubbed off on him somewhat. "If I'm the reason that you get to stop and smell the roses, then I'm glad. We'll have lots of fun, I promise you."

"I know we will. Just being with you is fun for me." He stopped and looked at me. "I mean that, Orla. I've never enjoyed anyone's company more in my life."

Sighing, I wished this would last much longer than it could. "Me too, Warner. I mean that. Just being with you makes me happy."

He looked at me for a moment. My lips trembled as my heart raced, hoping he would kiss me. But then he sighed and turned away. "We should get going. We can get something to eat, and then I'll take you to check out that piano bar I told you about."

One little kiss won't take too much time.

But he was off, and I knew the kiss would have to wait until later. It was insane how much my body craved the man. Every cell in me screamed out for his touch. I'd never felt such sexual frustration.

I wasn't usually the one to make the first move. Perhaps it was from a fear of rejection. I had no idea, but I always waited for the man to make it.

I followed Warner as he took a path through the trees,

making it impossible to walk beside him. I thought about why I didn't just kiss him myself instead of waiting for him to do it.

What did it matter if I did it?

I wasn't home where I would have to worry about my reputation. No one would be telling anyone I knew that I had made the first move. There wasn't anything I would have to live down or feel ashamed of doing.

And why did I feel that kissing him first would be a shameful act anyway?

Was I not a liberated woman? Did I not believe in the equality of the sexes? What sort of woman was I?

I couldn't blame it on being shy, as I was far from shy. I couldn't blame it on being prudish, as I wasn't that either. Then it clicked as I heard my mother's voice in my head.

A lady waits for the man to offer her his kiss—not the other way around.

Is that really the only thing stopping me from kissing this man? Those long-ago spoken words seemed so insignificant compared to the broad shoulders and the manly scent wafting off him.

But I found it hard to stray from my mother's brainwashing. I didn't go for it as we made our way to his truck. I didn't go for it after we'd eaten a dinner of fish and chips. And I didn't go for it while we sat, singing along with others at the piano bar.

"I've got friends in low places, where the whisky runs and the beer chases the blues away," I sang loudly as the beer had done its job limiting my inhibitions.

"How do you know the words to so many of these songs, Orla?" Warner asked, then took a swig of his beer.

"I listen to American country music at home." Sipping some of my Guinness, I watched his eyes light up and loved the way that looked.

"That's my favorite genre of music." Placing the mug on the

table, he leaned in close enough for me to smell the beer on his warm breath. "We've got a lot in common."

"That we do." It was a common theme throughout the night. First, we kept ordering the same foods. I'd ordered my food while Warner had gone to the men's room to freshen up. And when he got back, he ordered exactly what I had. He'd even gotten a sweet tea just. Although when I'd looked around at the other tables, I saw that many of the other patrons also had the same beverage in front of them.

Tea and Texas seemed to go hand in hand the same way a pint and Ireland do. As I looked into his eyes, I saw more in them than I'd ever seen in anyone's eyes. I saw hope, excitement, even frailty.

Gulping, I realized a knot had formed in my throat. Without even meaning to, I felt empathy for the man, remembering how he'd lost his parents. Of course his heart would be affected by that. But the hope in his eyes told me that it was beginning to grow larger than the vulnerability and fear he had become so comfortable with.

At the end of the night, as he walked me to my room, we held hands, and I leaned my head against his arm. "That was fun, Warner. Thank you for coming up with all these fun things to do. I truly appreciate it. If you want to see me tomorrow—"

"I do," he quickly interrupted.

I laughed, loving how open he was with me. "Well then, let me make the plans. You should get a break from making them for at least one day."

"I don't mind making them for you." We stopped in front of my room, and he pulled me around to face him. "I love spending time with you. You make all the plans you want for tomorrow, and I'll give you all the time you care to spend with me."

Running my hands up his arms, I moved them around his neck, clasping them together behind his head. "What a lucky girl I am." I bit my lower lip as I looked into his eyes. "I'll have to really give it some thought if I'm going to come close to comparing my date to the ones you've taken me on."

"I'll love anything you decide to do, I can assure you of that. Hell, I'd be happy doing absolutely nothing. As long as it's with you, I'm good."

"Easy to please. I like that in a man." I liked everything about Warner. "There are lots of things to like about you, Mr. Nash."

"As there are you, Orla Quinn." He licked his lips, and I was sure he was going to lean in for a kiss.

My lips pulsed as I waited for him to lower his to mine. I'd never wanted anything so badly in my life. I'd freely give my lips and mouth to his. And I knew I would never want the kiss to end.

"I'm excited," I said as my heart pounded inside my chest, "to start making plans for us for tomorrow."

"Good." He licked his lips again, and this time his gaze moved to mine—finally.

Come on, Warner—kiss me!

I had no idea what was holding him back, but I had the feeling that he might be worried about moving too fast with me. The thing was, we didn't have that much time left.

If we were going to get to the good stuff, someone had to open that door.

Not you, Orla Quinn. Let the man make the first move. My mother's voice rang inside my head.

But she wasn't there. My eyes cut first to one side and then to the other as I checked out the hallway to be sure it was empty. I couldn't have any spies from Kenmare catch me.

With no one in the hallway save us, I leaned in, closing the gap between us, and to my bliss, Warner leaned in too. We met in the middle, our lips barely touching.

Pure fire filled my veins as adrenaline shot through me like a bolt of lightning. My lips parted, my tongue teased his lower lip. Then he pushed me back against the door, kissing me hard.

The kiss went from zero to one hundred in less than a second.

My nails moved down his back as my feet came off the floor, wrapping around his waist. I felt his cock throbbing as it grew in size against my sex.

My panties soaked as his kiss took me completely under. I'd never been so utterly lost in a kiss. I was sure that sex with Warner was going to be the best I would ever have—and all this from just a kiss.

Well, it was a bit more than that. Whatever it was, it was extraordinary. And when he pulled his mouth away from mine, we both panted so loudly that it sounded as if we'd just made love for hours. "See you tomorrow then, Orla."

Unwrapping my legs from their place around him, I felt shaky when I stood on my feet. "See you tomorrow then, Warner. Goodnight."

I turned and ran the card through to open my door. When I looked back, he was stepping onto the elevator. As I staggered into my room, drunk on his kiss alone, I knew I was in for a rough parting when the day came for me to leave.

But by God, I will not miss out on this experience.

13

WARNER

I'D BEEN SITTING IN MY OFFICE, WORKING ON THE COMPUTER FOR more than half the day, before a knock came to my door. "It's Orla."

"Come in." I closed my computer, more than ready to stop working so I could spend time with her. The kiss last night had left me in a haze of bliss, and my dreams had been off the charts.

She came in, closing the door behind her. "How's your day been?"

"It's been pretty boring without you in it." I got up, went right to her, then pulled her into my arms, unable to keep my lips off of hers.

Tilting her head up, she looked at me with shining eyes as her lips parted. As our mouths collided, stars filled my head, and heat swept through my body. I was so glad we'd gotten that first kiss out of the way.

Holding her close, I felt her heart beating as if she'd just run five miles. I eased out of the kiss but didn't let her go—I needed to feel her body against mine.

She put her hand on my chest and looked at me with a blush on her cheeks. "Wow. I don't know how you do that. But—wow."

"I didn't do anything. That was all you."

There wasn't a doubt in my mind that the sex between us would be like nothing I'd had before. And I was more than eager to get to it.

If we'd already popped the cork on that, I would've cleared my desk and laid her out on it. But this was not the place for us to have sex for the first time. I did care about this girl, after all.

Placing her hands on my chest, she pushed me gently. "Warner, I've got to go. I just wanted to tell you to come up to my room in about an hour. I've got something special planned for you. It will be all set up by then."

In her room? Yes!

"So, the date will be in your room?" I had to make sure I'd heard her right.

"Yes. Is that okay with you?" She looked at me with concern. "If you think it'll make you uncomfortable..."

"No," I interrupted, "it's not that. I was just making sure, is all. Should I bring something? Wine? Beer? Sweet tea?"

"I've got it covered, baby."

Shaking my head, I had to let her know that that was not the endearment for me. "You can call me babe, but baby isn't a thing a man likes to be called." I furrowed my brow and puffed my chest, trying to make myself look extra manly.

She laughed, just as I'd hoped. "No? Well, how about babe, then?" She nodded. "Well, I'll see you in an hour, babe."

Pulling at my lower lip between my teeth as I watched her walk out the door, I knew tonight was going to be the night where we took things to the next level. "I've gotta shower," I mumbled to myself.

I headed to the front desk. "Jeannie, do we have a free room?" I asked.

"We have four of them, Mr. Nash."

"Great. I've gotta freshen up. Hook me up."

Tapping away at the computer, she finally handed me the keycard. "Here you go. It's room three-eighty-one."

"Great." I headed to the boutique to buy something to wear. It took me no time to find a set of cream-colored linen pants that fit loosely and a shirt that matched exactly. A pair of grey flip flops finished my laid-back look.

Once in my room, I took a shower, washed and conditioned my hair, then got dressed. With the important stuff done, I found I had about ten minutes to spare. Instead of combing my hair the way I usually did, I ran my fingers through it, leaving it on the wilder side.

Before leaving the room, I checked myself out in the full-length mirror and liked what I saw. "She's gonna love you."

Now that I had a room for the night, I could stay with Orla as late as she'd let me. But I was hoping for an all-nighter as I headed to her room.

Knocking on her door, I felt a little nervous. All that fell away as I found myself trying not to laugh when she opened the door, her mouth gaping as she looked me up and down. "You're a beave, Warner."

"A beave?" I wasn't sure what she meant by that. "You don't like my casual look?"

She grabbed my hand, pulling me inside, then closing the door. "I don't want that horrible Mona seeing you like this. She'd charge ya like a mad bull, she would. I love the way you look. A beave is like a sexy beast."

"Ah, a sexy beast." *I like that.* "Well, thank you."

She looked cute as hell in a pale green tracksuit and a white apron from one of our restaurants, Essence. The name was embroidered in the middle at the top of the apron, covering her chest. "And you look adorable." Some amazing smells were wafting around the room, and I spotted two silver domes on the small dining table. "You got us take-out?"

"Better than that. I cooked it for us. Chef Giovani allowed me to use his kitchen during the slow hours today."

"You're something else, Orla." I was shocked that she'd talked one of our chefs into letting her do that. But then again, she must've told him she was cooking it for me. "I can't wait to dig in."

"Great." She pulled the domes off the plates and introduced me to the meal she'd prepared for us. "We have Shepard's pie as the main course, with a side of cheesy Guinness bread. And Irish Barmbrack for dessert. I also made a pitcher of Irish martinis." She filled each martini glass, and then we took our seats.

I'd had Shepard's pie before, but hers was much better. "Yum," I moaned as I chewed the first bite. "This tastes amazing."

Smiling from ear to ear, she clapped her hands. "Yeah? I'm so glad you like it."

The bread was light and fluffy and tasted like heaven. "Oh, my God, this is good too!"

Pride radiated around her. "The bread is one of my specialties. I make it at the bar too and serve it in wee chucks."

"Lucky me, to have such a good cook as my girl." I winked at her then took a sip of the drink. "It's sort of like a dirty martini. but there's something else. It's barely there, but it's there."

"I swirled the chilled pitcher with Irish whisky before pouring in the other ingredients. Placing her elbows on the table, she gazed at me. "I like that you're taking the time to experience all the flavors."

"Eat, don't just watch me eat." I waved my fork at her. "I love every last thing you've made, Orla."

"Wait till you taste the dessert." She took her first bite, making me happy not to be eating alone.

Picking up the dessert that resembled banana bread, I sniffed it. "Almost smells like pumpkin pie. With extra cinnamon. And there's a hint of whisky, too. And are those raisins I see?"

"You've nearly told me every ingredient in it, Warner. Bravo for you and your brilliant nose."

"I had no idea I had a sharp nose until now." Her compliments made me happy. She had a way of making me feel special. She had a way of making me want to be more than I was.

"After dinner, my plan is to watch movies and just hang out. Would that be okay with you?"

Being that we'd be lying on the bed to watch the movies, it was more than okay with me. "I'm game."

Her head tilted as she looked at me with wide eyes. "And that means what, exactly?"

"Yeah, it's cool with me if we do that." I didn't want to sound too eager and start jumping up and down—even though that was precisely what I wanted to do. "Chilling and watching movies sounds good to me, baby."

Smiling, she went back to eating her food. "Good. I was afraid you'd find it a boring way to spend an evening. But the truth is that I spend five nights out of seven working at the bar. On my days off, I like to enjoy some quiet time, watching movies and just hanging out at home."

"So, you're showing me a typical night for you when you're not working." I liked how she wanted to show more of herself to me. I also hoped to see more of her than I'd seen so far. More skin, to be specific.

"I am. It's funny. You showed me how you spend your nights, cooking on your patio then sitting in your comfy chair watching television. You and I do the same things." She sighed. "We like the same foods, too. I've been noticing."

"You bring out different things in me. Do I bring out anything different in you?" I finished off the last bit of the meal before going for the dessert.

"I have noticed that you bring out something I call hominess. Like, I want to cook for you. I've rarely cooked for anyone I've dated. And I've never just hung out and watched movies with any of the men I've seen either. I preferred to go out with them. Sometimes we'd go back to their place but never to mine. But you—you, I would take home."

"Wow. I would be one you would take home. A high compliment indeed." It felt amazing to hear her say that. To hear that I ranked better than any other man she'd been with.

"My parents would adore you." She put her fork down, picking up her drink, and holding it between her hands as if it were a cup of coffee. "Pity."

Trying to change the topic, I took a bite of the dessert. "So much better than banana bread."

A smile curved her pink lips. She didn't have much makeup on at all, and still, she was the most beautiful woman I'd ever seen. Her auburn hair was pulled up into a loose bun on top of her head, with tendrils falling in spiral curls here and there. She wasn't even trying to be gorgeous, and yet she still was.

"It's got a higher moisture content than banana bread." She finally took a sip of the drink, then put it down. "Would you terribly mind if I took a quick shower? I've been cooking, and the kitchen was hot as Hades."

"I wouldn't mind at all. As a matter of fact, I'll clean this up and leave it in the hall for guest services to pick up." The thought of her coming back smelling fresh and clean enticed me to no end.

"Good. I'll just finish up then and get to the shower." She took a few more bites, then placed her napkin on her plate. "You can find something you'd like to watch while I'm showering."

I would find something we could watch together. Something romantic, and maybe even a little funny. I loved her laugh. "Will do."

As she got up to make her way to the bathroom, she suddenly stopped and went to the dresser. "I can't come back out here with nothing more than a towel on. I need to take my clothes in there with me."

"You're taking the fun out of this for me." I teased her.

She pulled out a set of dark green silk pajamas, then put them back into the drawer. Then she picked up a dress that was much too fancy to wear to lie around and watch TV, but then put it back. "This is crazy. I can't figure out what to wear."

"The silk pajamas," I said quickly. "What I've got on is close to pajamas too."

"It is, right?" She took the green slips of fabric back out of the drawer, then discreetly took out a pair of matching panties and a bra.

"Orla, a bra with pajamas?" I shook my head. "You don't have to wear that. If it makes you feel any better, I don't have any underwear on."

She erupted in laughter and ran to the bathroom. "You're so bad."

I gathered up the dishes and placed them in the hall before going to lie on the bed, grabbing the remote and searching for the perfect movie for us.

I wonder how long she's going to make me wait.

Orla had to know that tonight would be the night. We were going to be adults lying in a bed together, watching a romantic comedy. That's what happens when couples do something like that, especially if the chemistry between them was out of this world.

It would almost be unnatural if we didn't end up having sex at this point.

I found the perfect movie, then got up to fold the blankets back, propping and fluffing the pillows. I grabbed the pitcher of martinis and our glasses, then refilled them and placed them on either side of the bed on the nightstands.

Looking up at the overhead light, I decided it had to go, so I jumped up to turn it off. I only kept on one of the lamps nearest to me.

With the mood set, I picked up my glass and took a drink of the tasty cocktail, waiting for my girl to join me on the bed.

14

ORLA

Pinching my cheeks to make them rosier, I scrunched my damp curls with my hands, then shook my head to get my hair to fall into place. Surveying my appearance, I deemed it cute and somewhat cuddly.

I hope he likes to cuddle after sex.

I'd always wanted a man who liked to cuddle instead of rolling over to sleep or completely get out of bed to shower right away.

It always bothered me when the man I'd just had sex with couldn't get to the shower fast enough to wash off what he must've perceived as a foul stench.

Sex did have a distinct smell. And mixing all those fluids together could cause an unpleasant smell at times. But the hurry to wash? Rude, in my opinion. And if the smell was so bad, why not invite your lover to shower with you?

Although I'd never had a cuddler, I always wanted one. I closed my eyes and wished for that. One never knew when the wish fairy would be listening.

As I went into the room, I found Warner had turned all the

lights off, save the one next to him. It illuminated him, making him appear ethereal. "You look fresh."

"You look comfy." I went around the bed to get in on the other side, taking notice of the television screen. "Oh good, you picked out a movie. What's it about?" I crawled over the bed to get right next to him, making sure our shoulders touched, as well as our legs. His masculine presence alone was enough to excite me.

"It's a romantic comedy." He picked up the remote and started the movie. After he put it down, ran his arm around my shoulders, pulling me close to him and sniffing my hair. "You smell good too."

"So do you." I inhaled his scent and sighed. "This is nice already."

"I agree." Snuggling down a bit, he pulled me towards him. "Let's see if this movie interests us."

I didn't care what the movie was about. I wanted to enjoy being with him. We had four more days and nights together before I had to go home. I wanted to make the most of each one of them.

As we watched the movie, a scene came on, where the couple talked about birth control before they had sex. I took it as a sign to let Warner know that I was covered. "I'm on the pill too, by the way."

"Good to know." He kissed the top of my head as I moved to lay my head on his broad chest. "I'd hate to send you back to Ireland knocked up with a half American baby."

"I'd hate it if you did that too." I eased my hand down his thick upper thigh. The movie was alright, but it was him I was interested in.

He ran his hand up and down my spine. "You know that I'm not the type of man who would leave you high and dry with a bun in your oven, right?"

Just knowing that was good enough for me. I believed him. "You are honorable."

"And you're respectable." His fingers moved along the top of my bottom.

I began unbuttoning his shirt, moving my hand over his muscular torso as I went from the bottom to the top. Rolling over on top of him, I pushed his shirt open and gazed at his finely structured body. "And you are well-built."

He reached out and began unbuttoning my shirt. My body quivered as he moved up closer and closer to my breasts with each button he undid. He pushed the shirt off my shoulders, sending it to puddle on top of the blanket behind me. "You're well-endowed." He cupped my breasts in his big hands. "A bit more than a handful—perfectly sized for me."

I laughed. "Maybe God created me just for you, Mr. Nash."

"Maybe he did." He drew me to him. "Let's see if you taste as delicious as you look."

My breath came out in a ragged wave as he kept pulling me until I was lying flat on him, our mouths coming together in a soft kiss. Our bare chests, flesh against flesh, only added more heat to the kiss. Feeling his skin on mine made me unbearably hot.

Every muscle in his torso rippled as he held me tightly then rolled over so he was on top. Although our pants were between us, I felt him growing larger as he grounded himself against my sex.

I wrapped my legs around him, urging him to continue his movements as he made my juices flow within me like wine. I moved my hands over his muscular back, running them up and down the small hills and valleys, moaning all the while.

His mouth left mine as he kissed a line along my neck, sending chills all through me. My nipples went rock hard. Warner growled, "You like that, huh?" He kissed a line down to one breast, then licked it a few times before sucking it into his mouth.

"Yes," I whimpered as my body arched. "I like it very much." His hair was soft as feathers as I moved my hands through it while he nipped and sucked my breast.

His mouth moved, kissing down the middle of my stomach, and then he took the elastic waistband of my pajama bottoms and pulled them off.

Panting, I watched him as he moved backward on his hands and knees until he was off the bed and stood, dropping his pants to the floor. His erection was huge, making my mouth water instantly. It had length and girth, and I felt like an extremely lucky woman to be staring at him. He moved back to the bed, crawling up between my spread legs.

His eyes on mine, he whispered, "I'm going to make this a night you will never forget."

A shudder ran through me. "Please do." I didn't want to forget anything about Warner Nash—not ever.

One hand moved up my inner thigh, making me tense. He licked his lips before kissing me in the most intimate of areas. I gasped as my fingers curled into the bed, pulling the fitted sheet from the top corners.

Moving my arms to rest my elbows on the bed, I held up my upper body. I had to watch him. He kissed me so softly it felt as if butterflies' wings were beating against me. His tongue tapped my clit, and my head fell back as I moaned, "Yes! That feels amazing!"

His teeth grazed me, then he nipped at my flesh, creating a wave that moved inside me. It soared until it found its way to a crashing point, leaving me in a state of ecstasy I'd never been in before.

His tongue darted into me as he pushed my legs wider for

him. He devoured me, and I couldn't stop the orgasm that raged within.

Shaking, I watched him as he kissed his way up my body. He pushed me gently, forcing me to lie back on the bed. "You taste like heaven, baby." He kissed me, his tongue running around mine.

The taste of me on his tongue turned me ravenous—I felt animalistic. I grabbed the back of his neck, kissing him hard as I moved my tongue around his. And then I felt him as he moved his body down, slowly, the head of his thick male member touching the edge of my canal.

I knew it was going to hurt. He was much bigger than any man I'd ever been with. Pushing himself into me a little at a time, he gave me time to stretch and accommodate him. He took his time with me, and I was grateful for it.

Once he was fully inside of me, he pulled his mouth off of mine. "You okay?"

Looking into those crystal blue eyes of his, I nodded. "I'm more than okay."

He eased back out, then back in again. "Good?"

"Great."

Smiling, he moved inside of me as we gazed into each other's eyes. I rested my hands on his biceps, loving the way the muscles moved with him.

I pulled my knees up, letting him sink deeper inside me, and closed my eyes as he touched places that had never been touched before.

He moaned quietly, "You're so tight."

"You're so big."

"I could do this forever," he leaned in to whisper to me.

His hot breath against my neck stirred me even more—which I didn't think was possible. It was like magic, what this man did to me. Everywhere he touched, flames ignited. Every breath he exhaled, I inhaled. I wanted to feel every bit of him that I possibly could.

He rolled over, putting me on top and pushing me in a sitting position.

He held me from the waist as I started grinding against him. Moving my hands over his firm pecs, I looked down. Warner was a gorgeous man on a bad day, but he turned into a Greek God during sex.

My hands moved to caress his cheeks. A five o'clock shadow had grown in, making his face a little rough. I liked it. "You're so masculine." I leaned down and kissed his cheek, liking the rough way it felt.

"And you're so feminine." His hands moved over my raised bottom, cupping both cheeks, guiding me to the speed he wanted.

The feel of him inside me was a thing I would want forever. As the thought of that not being an option ran through my head, one tear slipped from my eye.

He pushed me up, not missing anything. Running his thumb over the tear that had escaped, his gaze focused on mine. "Why the tears?"

I shook my head. I didn't want to talk about it. "This is beautiful." It was beautiful, that was no lie.

His lips curved into a smile. "It is beautiful."

"And it's special."

"It is." He ran his hand over my cheek. "Never think that this is just sex between us, Orla. It's so much more than that."

And yet, it cannot last.

Closing my eyes, I didn't want any more tears to fall. I didn't want to sully this magical moment by crying over what could never be. *Just enjoy what we have now and don't think about the future.*

Focusing on the pleasure, I let all other thoughts leave my

head. Warner moved us once again, this time, so we were lying on our sides. Still connected, we faced each other. He took control of the pace and I threw one leg over his thigh.

Running his hand through my hair, his eyes shone brightly before he leaned in and kissed me. It felt like I was in the middle of a fairy tale. The prince had rescued me, and now he was turning me into his princess.

There hadn't been enough time for love to grow but damned if it didn't feel like love to me. A love so deep and strong that it felt it had always been there. True or not, it felt real to me.

The kiss grew in passion, and Warner's desire grew as well. He turned me onto my back, then made a low groan as he moved faster, thrusting harder. "I need you."

Putting my hands on his shoulders, I held onto him, so his hard thrusts didn't push me up the bed and away from him. "You've got me."

Faster and harder he moved, until I couldn't take it anymore. The friction had taken me to another level that proved to be the breaking point for me. An orgasm came crashing through my body, ripping away anything that wasn't pure, unadulterated pleasure.

My orgasm sent him into one as well, and he growled like a tiger as he came inside of me. My head felt light, my body pulsed, and my heart felt as if it was about to pound right out of my chest.

Our heavy breathing filled the room. He eased his body down on top of me. His heart pounded against mine. Our skin was slick with perspiration—I'd never felt happier in my entire life.

The world began to bleed back in as the euphoria receded. "Was that real or my imagination?" I asked.

He chuckled, making his body vibrate. "That was extremely real, baby." Pulling his head up, he kissed my lips lightly. "I think you and I both know how we'll be spending the remainder of your trip."

As I ran my hands over his back, desperately trying to memorize how he felt, I knew we'd end up spending more time like this than in any other way. And I also knew that doing so would only build our connection. But I didn't care that it would have to end. We had to have this. We had to know that love like this did exist. Even if we couldn't have it together, we would know that we could have it.

"Thank you, Warner."

He looked at me with raised brows. "For what, exactly?"

"For showing me that I can feel much deeper than I knew I could."

He smiled crookedly. "Yeah, you've done that for me too. I've never let myself go like that before. And man did it make a difference."

"Me too." I'd been holding back and hadn't realized it.

But I wasn't sure I would be able to give my all to another man. And that was because Warner was making a place for himself in my heart.

Moving off me, he lay on his side. He pulled me back to him, spooning with me. With his arm wrapped around my waist, he kissed the side of my neck. "We should get a little sleep before we do that again."

He's a cuddler! Yes!

I placed my hand on the one he rested on my stomach. "Night, sweet prince."

"For you, I'll be a prince, my Irish princess." It took no time for his breathing to fall into a steady rhythm, letting me know he was fast asleep.

My eyes had remained open, thinking about life as he held me the way I'd always wanted a man to hold me. Life without him in it. Life without ever knowing if I would see him again.

I didn't know if I wanted a life like that. But it wasn't entirely up to me.

I couldn't leave my family, and I knew he felt the same way about his family and their business. Nothing had ever been more hopeless than our connection. We may as well have been from two separate planets.

Perhaps we were destined to be stars that collided, then burst into flaming fragments, destroying one another. *Lord, I hope that's not true.*

15

WARNER

THE FIRST THING I FELT IN THE MORNING WAS THE SOFT SKIN THAT lay beneath my hand. The discovery woke me up with a smile on my face. My eyes flew open.

Orla lay in my arms, her auburn curls a mess on the pillow, tickling my nose.

We'd woken three times during the night, making love each time. I'd never done anything like that. I'd also never felt such a strong connection to anyone before.

It was evident that I'd worn her out completely, as she didn't even stir as I slipped out of bed. Knowing I had to let her rest, I pulled on my clothes and left her to slumber.

I had to get home to get ready for the day. The sun had barely begun peeking over the horizon as I drove home. It was early, and very little traffic got in my way.

Since Orla had gone out of her way to prepare me a meal, I was going to make one for her. And that meant I'd be bringing her to my place. I prayed she would want to spend the night with me there, too. Sure, it would mean that I'd need to replenish my electrolytes and take some vitamins to be able to perform as well as I had the night before, but I was up for the challenge.

As soon as I got home, I got on my computer and put in the order of groceries I would need to make Orla a real Texas barbeque dinner. On our way back home later in the day, I'd stop by the store to pick up the order.

After a shower, I put on a pair of jeans, a pearl snap shirt, and a pair of cowboy boots. I wanted to give Orla the real Texas experience. As I walked out the door, I decided to take her shopping at my favorite western wear store and buy her an outfit, including a pair of cowboy boots. At least she'd have something unique to take back home with her. Something that would always remind her of me. Plus, we could take some pictures together, wearing matching outfits. I'd never even wanted to do a thing like that before.

Orla made me want to be someone I never knew I wanted to be. But I liked the way I felt, and I hoped I would continue feeling this high even after she had to leave.

When I pulled into my parking spot at the resort, I found Patton getting out of his car. Waving, I got out of the truck. "Morning, bro."

"Moring, Warner." He looked me up and down. "No suit today?"

"Nah." I let him catch up to me, and then we walked together. "I'm taking a date home today and making barbeque for her, so I thought I'd dress the part of a typical Texas cowboy."

His eyes went wide. "*You're* taking a date to your *home*?"

"I know I've said in the past that I don't like taking girls home, but this one is different."

"How?"

"I don't know—she feels more real to me. I mean…she's got a good soul and heart. She's here from Ireland, and she'll only be here for a few more days. So I'm taking her home today after work, and then I think I'm going to take the rest of the week off. I want to show her around, at least a little of our state."

"Time off?" He chuckled. "Who the hell are you?"

"I know, right?" I had to laugh too. "This is not me. I've been saying that to myself all morning. Hell, I'm even going to take her shopping today to get her some cowgirl duds so we'll match."

"That's sweet." He bumped my shoulder with his. "When's the wedding?"

"Ha, ha." I just shook my head. "We know this isn't a permanent thing. She's got family back home, one she's not about to leave. And you know my deal—the resort and all."

"You know, there's something nice about having a deadline," he pointed out. "You both know it's going to end, and so, you're living it up while you can."

"Yeah." Patton had always gotten me. "You get it."

"I do." We walked through the lobby doors. It was early, and not many people were moving about yet. "Just try to stay open-minded here, Warner. I like seeing you this way—all smiles and thinking about someone else."

"I'm gonna try." My stomach felt empty, and I knew I had to get something to eat. "You want to join me for breakfast?"

"Yeah, I haven't eaten anything yet. Alexis wasn't up when I left. It's her day off, and I wasn't about to wake her or the kids up, so I slipped out without making myself anything to eat."

We headed to the breakfast room, where a spread was laid out each morning for our staff and guests. I grabbed a plate, then went for all the protein I could get. Bacon, three kinds of sausage, scrambled eggs, and a ton of fresh baby spinach. When I sat down with Patton at a small table, he eyed my heaping plate.

I just shrugged. "I had quite the workout."

"Last night or this morning?" He winked at me, knowing

what kind of workout I was talking about.

"Both." I took a big bite of the eggs that I'd mixed with the spinach.

One of the waitstaff came by with a coffee pot and filled the cups that had been waiting on the table. "Moring, bosses." She pulled some creamers and sugar packets out of her apron pocket. "Here you go. Enjoy."

Gulping down the food, I smiled. "Thanks, Joy."

"You're welcome." She left us to tend to other guests.

"You know something, Warner," Patton said, "you've always been so friendly with people. It's always perplexed me how you find it easy to speak to people so easily—you've got this emotional intelligence that's out of the roof—and yet, you've never managed to have even a semi-decent relationship with a member of the opposite sex. Until now, it seems. And this isn't even something that can last."

I wasn't trying to psychoanalyze myself. "You know, I'm not going to worry about it right now."

"Because you're having fun with this Irish lass?"

"Yes." I picked up a piece of bacon, devouring it.

I wasn't going to waste my time with Orla trying to become my own therapist. It merely wasn't important to me at the moment.

What really mattered to me was that I now knew that I could be this guy—the guy who adores his girl and plans his day around her. A guy who isn't afraid that love can't last or that it can be stolen from him so quickly that it boggles the mind. For now, I was the trusting type with no worries.

"There you are," came a lilting voice from behind me. Her hands moved over my shoulders, and then I felt warm lips pressed against my cheek. "I woke up, and you were gone. I'm famished and had to get up to get something to eat."

Patton's eyes lit up as he looked at the woman who stood behind me. "Ah, you must be my brother's Irish lass."

"Orla Quinn." She extended her hand, and he shook it. "And which brother are you?"

"I'm the second oldest, Patton. It's a pleasure to meet you, Orla. I've got to tell you that you've made a remarkable difference in my brother."

"A good one, I hope." She slipped into the chair next to mine and the waitress filled the empty cup in front of her with steaming hot coffee. Orla looked at her with a smile. "Morning, Joy. Thank you so much."

"I think it's a good one," Patton agreed.

16

ORLA

With a cold beer in hand and my boots propped up on the outdoor coffee table, I couldn't imagine a better way to spend the night. The smell of barbeque wafted through the cool air, and I felt perfectly content. "Warner, that is the most tantalizing smell I believe I have ever had the pleasure of sniffing in my life."

"Hickory smoke is one of the best smelling smokes there is." He picked up his beer then came to sit next to me on the comfy couch.

As he took the seat, I smelled the smoke on him and moaned as I leaned in, sniffing his neck. "My goodness, you should find a way to bottle that smell. You could sell a ton of it as men's cologne."

Laughing, he asked, "Does it turn you on?"

"In so many ways." My head felt light as I inhaled him. "I think I could kiss every last inch of you, if only just to taste that smoke on your skin." I shook my head. "Oh, that sounds a little like something a cannibal would say, doesn't it?"

"A little." He took a drink of the long-neck beer bottle, then placed it on the table beside him. "At least you didn't say you'd like to bite me all over to taste the smoke on my skin. Now *that* would've been creepy."

Earlier in the evening, he'd taken me on a shopping spree to buy me some western clothing. My shirt and his had the same type of buttons—which he called pearl snaps. He'd picked out some blue jeans for me as well, and the larger bottoms on the legs made for better covering my new cowboy boots. I looked like a real cowgirl, and now I was about to eat like one.

No one had ever gone to so much trouble—or expense—for me. I sort of liked being pampered. *Who am I kidding? I love being pampered.*

"The appetizers are just about ready." He wiggled his thick, dark brows at me. "Get ready for something spicy."

He'd piqued my curiosity. "I saw you putting something on the grill that was wrapped in bacon. Is that the spicy appetizer you speak of?"

"It is. They're called wraps. It's a hollowed-out jalapeno filled with cream cheese then wrapped with bacon. It's a staple at Texas barbeques."

"You're certainly giving me the star treatment here, cowboy."

His eyes searched mine for a moment. "I like it better when you call me your sweet prince."

Caressing his cheek, which he'd skipped shaving this morning, my heart melted. He'd referred to what I'd called him the night before. "Ah, and my sweet prince you are."

His gaze broke from mine as he looked to one side. Smoke billowed out of the grill, and he jumped up to see to it. "I think the wraps are burning!"

As soon as he lifted the lid on the grill, the flames shot up. "Bacon grease will catch fire." I stayed on the couch and out of his way.

Masterfully, he grabbed a pair of huge oven mitts and slipped them over his hands. They went all the way up to his elbows. Taking a long pair of tongs, he shouted, "Grab the platter for me, please."

Hopping up, I grabbed the empty platter near him and held it out. He quickly filled it with the wraps, and I was surprised to see very little char on them. "Seems you got them out in the nick of time."

"It's important not to walk away from food when you're grilling." He closed the lid and the smoke soon stopped billowing out of the hole on top of the lid.

"I can see why." My beer was nearly empty, and so was his. I ambled over to the ice chest that was cooling our beer, grabbed two more, and took them to the table where he'd placed the platter of appetizers.

"I'll be right back. I've got a peach cobbler in the oven." He left me alone with the food.

I decided to try one before he could witness my reaction to the spicy thing. Picking up the smallest one, I popped it whole into my mouth. To my surprise, it wasn't spicy at all, and it tasted phenomenal.

But after swallowing it, something started happening to my tongue. At the very back, a slight burning sensation began, and it kept getting warmer and warmer. I took a swig of the cold beer but it didn't help at all.

Warner came back outside to find me with my tongue sticking out, trying to let the cool breeze to put an end to the ever-growing warmth. "Let me guess, you tried a wrap?"

"Yes, and now my mouth is on fire."

He opened the bag of thickly sliced bread he'd placed on the table and handed me a piece. "Take a bite of this and let the bread sit on your tongue a minute before you chew it up and swallow it."

I did as he said, waiting for a moment before swallowing it. And it took away most of the heat. "Wow, that worked."

"The bread draws in the oil the pepper leaves behind." He popped one of the little fireballs into his mouth.

I waited for him to reach for a piece of bread, but he didn't. Instead, he did just the opposite, popping another spicy ball of fire into his mouth.

Flabbergasted, I asked, "It doesn't burn your mouth?"

Shaking his head, he said, "It does burn, but I like it."

"Ya like it?" I couldn't believe him. "How could anyone like their mouth feeling as if it were on fire?"

Shrugging, he took a drink of the beer before eating a third fiery treat. "Come on. Try another. You get used to the heat."

With the bread in my hand, I found one that seemed fairly small and took a small bite. "It's not that bad when I eat it in small increments. The taste is good. It's the heat I despise." But I found that taking a bite of the bread between bites of the pepper helped the war against heat.

Warner went to the crockpot of pinto beans and gave them a stir. "Beans are ready. I checked on the potato salad in the fridge while I was in the house. The salad and the cobbler are both ready. Now it's time to take the brisket off the pit and give it time to rest before I cut into it."

"Real American barbeque," I said as I rubbed my hands together in anticipation.

"No. Real *Texas* barbeque," he corrected me as I went along with him to remove the meat from the pit.

Smoke clouded what was lying on the grill inside. "I can't see a thing."

"Hang on." He waved one hand over the pit to push the smoke away, and there lay a black, completely charred block of what I assumed was meat. "Yeah! Now that's what I'm talking about."

"So, that's not burnt meat?" If I'd pulled that from my oven, I would've cried as I dumped it into the rubbish bin.

"No, ma'am. This is the way a great brisket is supposed to look when it's done properly." He picked up a stainless steel pan and placed it on the chopping block that ran along the front of the pit. Using his oven mitt-covered hands, he picked the meat up off the hot grill and placed it into the pan.

"I'll have to take your word for it." I took a drink from my beer, wondering if I would have to lie about loving the food he'd made for me.

"Come on inside. We'll eat in the dining room—a first for me."

"You really should invite people over, Warner. It's fun to entertain guests. And you're good at it." I didn't want to think of him going back to a life of solitude when I left. "At least, invite your family over now and then."

"I might just do that." His words made me happy.

I looped my arm through his. "Good. Now, let's enjoy this meal you've slaved over all day, shall we?"

17

WARNER

Three more nights—that's all I've got left with her.

With so little time left, I wasn't going to waste a single second. "I've taken the next four days off." I took one extra because I was sure that I wouldn't feel like working after I had to say goodbye.

She came out of the bathroom of my bedroom, wearing one of my t-shirts and looking cute as hell. "And what are our plans for today?" She reached for her bag, which she'd brought with her after I had asked her to spend the night with me on our barbeque date. She'd happily agreed. "I need to know what I should wear today."

"We're going to spend the night in a cabin by the river near the small town of Concan. It's a couple of hours from here, in the country." It was on the cool side, being January. "A light sweater and jeans would be good, I think." We'll take our time getting there, too. We'll find a place to have lunch and even dinner before getting there."

Taking her bag with her, she retreated back into the bathroom to get ready for our day. I loved the way she never argued about where we were going or huffed and said she didn't feel like doing what I planned for us.

I had no idea if that was because she was on vacation and didn't know what was possible or what the deal was—I simply loved it.

Our night had been another insanely sexual and unimaginably pleasurable one. The one thing I was sure of was that both of us were hitting it out of the ballpark in bed, and that was a thing no one could do forever.

The brevity of our romance enhanced everything. From the way food tasted to the way making love to each other felt, it was all enhanced by the knowledge that each day was a gift. We knew the gift would soon be gone.

Until that time came, we were both up for anything. Neither of us had ever experienced anything like this. And it made for another intimate connection, knowing that this was a first for each of us.

Gathering my clothes, I walked across the hallway to another bedroom with a bath attached so I could get cleaned up and ready to leave.

We'd found out earlier that morning when we'd tried to shower together that it wasn't an option for us. If we were together and naked, we were going to have sex—end of story.

When I made it back to my bedroom, I found her dressed and ready. "I'm good to go whenever you are."

I had to pack a bag for myself and took a piece of luggage from the closet. "Let me pack really quickly, then we're out of here, honey."

"Is there anything you want me to do while you're at it?" she asked.

"No, ma'am. I already loaded up the ice chest last night, and that's the only other thing we'll need for this trip—other than our packed bags."

It didn't take me long to pack, and then we were on our way to the hill country. The scenery along the way was some of the prettiest in the whole state of Texas. Orla looked out the window in awe. "I bet this is really gorgeous in the spring when everything is green."

"It is." We pulled up to the small cabin I'd rented online. "And here we are. Our little slice of paradise for the night."

She hurried out of the truck and ran around, looking at everything. "Hey, there's a hot tub on the porch back here!"

I entered the code into the lock system and gained access to the cabin. "Well, come on inside, and we'll check everything out."

She walked in through the front door, looking at the rustic furnishings and décor. "Is this how people used to live in the old days?"

"I think so. I mean, I think that's the look they're going for, so I'm sure it's kind of accurate. In the real old days, there was no air conditioning, and probably no running water or toilet." I was glad those days were long gone. I opened the back door and saw the hot tub on the back porch. "And no hot tubs either, I'm sure."

She sat on the bed at the back of the one-room cabin. Running her hand over the quilt, she said, "I like this very much, Warner. I feel like I'm getting to know your country even better."

It was hard not to want her as she sat on that bed. I sat down beside her, pointing up. "That skylight up there certainly wasn't part of the old world." But it would make our night so much better.

We both fell back on the bed, looking up at the sky that would soon be dark and full of stars. Our hands moved toward each other's until they touched. Holding hands while lying there, we looked at the sky until the sun faded away, turning the day into night.

We watched in silence until Orla whispered, "I could spend eternity doing just this."

I could spend eternity with only you.

My life would be so easy with Orla in it, I was sure of it.

"This must be what utopia is like." I rolled over to look at her. "I think you and I have found bliss."

She ran her hand over my cheek. "Your beard is coming in nicely, my prince."

I ran my hand through her curls. "Your hair just keeps getting silkier and silkier, my Irish princess."

"What if you and I were royalties in a past life? Ruling ancient Ireland together." She smiled at me, urging me to play along.

"Maybe we were. Maybe we share a past from so long ago that there aren't even any mentions of us in history books." I couldn't stand it any longer and kissed her lips. They looked plumper from all the kissing we'd done in the last days.

She would most definitely leave her mark on me when she left, and I was sure I would do the same for her. I moved my mouth to her neck, set on intentionally leaving my mark.

She loved it when I nibbled and kissed her neck. In no time, she was panting and trying to rid herself of her clothes and mine. In a panic of lust, we rushed to get each other undressed.

As I stood, I looked down at her as she lay on the bed with a smile on her face. Reaching down, I picked her up and held her high above me, then eased her body to graze against mine.

She wrapped her legs around me as I eased her down my long cock. Putting her arms around my neck, she kept her eyes on mine as I moved her up and down, up and down. "The blue of your eyes will be forever burned into my brain."

"As will your pale green ones. I'll never be able to see that color again without remembering your sensual persuasion." It didn't make sense to me that she didn't have her choice of men back home.

But maybe she didn't want any of them. Maybe she wanted a big strong American man to go home to.

Laughing to myself, I knew I was getting caught up in the fantasy. I had to remind myself of the reality of our situation. We'd only gotten this close this quickly because we knew we were running against the clock. There was no other reason.

We weren't lost mates from past lives. We weren't some ancient prince and princess who'd finally found one another after thousands of years apart.

She was simply a barmaid from Ireland, and I was just a businessman from Texas. We were nothing more than two strangers who had found each other for a moment in time and decided to take full advantage of that time they'd been given.

I began to wonder if life wouldn't be much better if everyone knew upfront the amount of time they had together. Even if it was seventy years, would it make their love grow deeper if they knew the exact day and time when they would be split apart?

That was the sort of thing being with Orla had done to me. It had made me into some sort of a philosopher, something I never was. I was a practical man. Not a dreamer. Practical.

But Orla and I were anything but practical. And I just had to hope that it wouldn't blow up in my face.

18

ORLA

The next morning, Warner had us taking off nice and early to our next destination. I fastened my seatbelt and asked, "So, where to now?"

"We're going to Fredericksburg to do some antiquing." He started up the truck, and off we went.

"Antiquing?" Nodding, I liked the idea of looking at old things people used to use in America. "That sounds good to me."

"Since you're so into finding out more about this place I call home, I thought that rummaging through some old stuff might be right up your alley. There are shops up and down both sides of the street and lots of little cafes, diners, and bars too."

"I've got to say that you Texans certainly know how to entertain." I'd never seen a place with so much to do. "I could stay here a month and still never get bored."

"Yeah, you should stay a month." He reached over, taking my hand and pulling it to his lips to leave a soft kiss there. "I'll be your guide around our state."

I wished I could take him up on his offer—I didn't want to

leave either. But Mum and Pop definitely needed me. "I wish I could, Warner. But my family needs me."

"I know." He rested my hand on his thigh, tracing his finger over the backs of my knuckles. "So, how'd you like the cabin by the river last night?"

"Well, you were there, so it was yet another amazing night. Thank you for taking me to that lovely place. I know I won't ever forget it." I also would never forget what we did there. Making love under the stars in the hot tub. The night had been chilly, the water warm, and we'd gotten lost in one another.

All I could say about making love with Warner was that it was as beautiful as it was pleasurable. He'd opened me up in ways I hadn't imagined possible.

"I'm glad you liked it." He caressed the back of my hand. "We'll be staying in another cabin near Fredericksburg tonight. It's in the woods." He winked at me. "Where no one will hear you scream."

"So, you're going to make me scream, are ya?" I laughed. "In pure ecstasy, I hope."

"Is there any other way, baby?" his drawl was exaggerated, and it sent a shiver down my spine.

"You're silly." I looked out the window as we wound through some exceptionally large hills. "It's so peaceful out here. Not a car in sight. It's as if we're all alone."

"The towns are ridiculously small around this part of the state, so the population isn't high at all. That leaves lots of room for feeling alone out here." He pointed out towards the window on my side. "Look down. This is the closest things we have to mountains around here."

"I can see that." I couldn't believe the drop-off and how close to the edge of the road it was. I grabbed the *oh shit* bar and hung on. "Way to show me what I'd been missing, babe." I had to close my eyes as the thought of falling down that steep ravine made its way through my mind, sparking my imagination with a fiery crash. "Just pay close attention to the road. This isn't the place to drive fast or take your eyes off the road."

"Scared, huh?" he chuckled as he gunned the engine to tease me. "Whoa!"

"Warner! Stop that!" I gave him a stern look so he would understand that I wasn't playing around.

"Sorry, baby. I'll stop screwing with you." He drove a lot better all the way down the hill.

When we got to the bottom, and the land was once again flat, I felt as if I should get out and kiss the ground. "You delight in teasing me, don't you?"

"It's pretty funny to watch you get so tense. I've driven these roads for many years. You've got nothing to worry about with me behind the wheel, baby."

"Have you never had an accident?" I cocked one brow at him because I was sure he'd had at least one with the way he drove.

"I don't like to talk about that while I'm driving."

"Tell me, please."

"I'll just say this. It was a very long time ago. I'd only had my license for two years, and it made me afraid to drive for about a year. My older brothers got tired of playing chauffeur to me and made me get back behind the wheel." He looked at me with serious eyes. "Believe me, I drive much better than I used to."

"But you still drive so fast." I wasn't sure how seriously he took driving. "And you tend to swerve in and out of traffic too."

"I was raised in Houston. And now I live in Austin. Dealing with traffic has always been a part of my driving. If you drive like an old lady, you'll have a hell of a time getting where you need to be in either of those cities."

"Where I come from, we don't have to rush around much at all. We tend to leave early enough so we don't have to speed to get to where we're going. Perhaps you should try doing that." I didn't want to worry all the time about Warner killing himself in a car wreck. "Promise me that you'll try to slow down at least a little from now on—even after I leave. I'd like to think that you're being careful. I'd like to think you're still alive, you know."

"I'll do it for you, Orla." He nodded, then kissed my hand again. "I won't make you worry about me after you leave."

"Good. And you can count on me not to drive crazy too." I liked that he would continue doing things for me—even after I was gone.

As we pulled into a small but busy town, I saw lots of cars parked on both sides of the streets. There were lots of people walking up and down the sidewalks. "Here we are." Warner parked the truck, and we got out to peruse the shops.

Hand in hand, we made our way from one shop to another, and I found bits of treasure in each. But I hadn't found anything to buy and take home. "There are so many cool things here. It's making it impossible for me to pick anything. If I had my own castle, I'd buy so many things to fill it with. But my tiny home can't hold much more than it already has. And I'm finding that a pity right now." There were cow skin rugs in so many colors and designs that my mind was boggled. Old fashioned bedroom furnishings, kitchen tables that looked like they were from old western mansions, and even old ironware for cooking.

The next shop we went into had a vast array of jewelry—all in big Texan style, of course. Warner picked out a necklace with a diamond-studded pendant and held it up. "This is the outline of Texas." He held it just above my breasts. "I'm getting it for you. It'll be a reminder that someone in Texas cares for you."

Happy to have something to remember him by, I nearly dropped dead when the store clerk told him the price for the trinket. "That's going to be three-thousand, sir."

"What?" I put my hand to my chest as my heart started beating like a bass drum. "Three-thousand what?"

Warner just chuckled. "Dollars. And don't think about the price—just think about the sentiment."

I couldn't wear the thing knowing it cost that much. "Don't get that for me, Warner. Get me something less expensive. What if I lose it or something? I'd hate myself forever if that happened."

"Don't lose it then. Be careful with it. Keep it somewhere safe." He took the necklace and walked behind me, placing it around my neck. "Like right here, for instance. Keep it close to your heart." After he fastened it, it fell into place. The pendant hung right between my breasts, over my heart. "That's where I belong—right there, next to your heart."

Next to my heart? No, you're inside of it, my love.

19

WARNER

It had finally arrived—our last night together. Early the next morning, she'd be leaving to go back to Ireland. I didn't want her to go. I didn't care if that was selfish of me. I wanted her to stay with me—forever.

I'd taken her to San Antonio to see the Riverwalk. I'd rented us a room in a hotel so we could sit on the balcony and see the lights from above.

There was so much more that I wanted to take her to see, but I'd run out of time. "I wish I hadn't waited so long before I decided to take you around the state."

She and I sat in the front of a gondola, a man with a long stick moving us through the San Antonio river. Darkness had just fallen, and both sides of the river had sprung to life. Mexican music played, people laughed, and the good-time vibe was everywhere.

"Let's not have any regrets about our time together. It moved at the pace it was supposed to." She leaned against me. "This is so festive. I adore it."

"Good." Wrapping my arm around her, I didn't want to ever

let her go. "Later, we'll go eat at one of these Mexican restaurants, and you can try out their specialty margaritas."

Her eyes glistened as she smiled. "Sounds delicious. And after that, what will we do?"

"I was hoping we'd go up to our room and make love like rabbits until we tire ourselves out." A sigh came out of me, as I was already missing her, and she wasn't even gone yet.

"That sounds like a good plan, babe."

The gondola pulled to the side. "Here's your stop. If you'll stop and stand in front of the mirror there, we'll take your photo for you. You can pick it up at the hotel's front desk and see if you'd like to buy it or not."

"Wow, that's so nice." Orla grabbed my face, pulling me down to her and kissing me as the photo was being taken. "Now, that's a keeper."

"I'll buy a copy for each of us." Taking her hand, I led her to one of the more festive restaurants. A mariachi band was playing next to the entrance. I tipped them as we passed. "Keep it happy, mi amigos."

My heart felt melancholy. I had to keep things as happy as possible, so I wouldn't start bawling like a baby. We only had one more night—I couldn't mess it up by sulking.

After being seated at a table near the water, Orla looked at the menu. "So, there're all these types of enchiladas. Are they good? And if so, which kind is the best?"

I looked at the menu and saw a sampler plate. "I think you should taste them all. Did you see the sampler plate, baby? It's got one of each enchilada and three kinds of mini tacos, a chalupa, rice and beans, guacamole, and sour cream, as well as pica de gallo."

"Warner, that's way too much food for me. I'll never eat all that." She just shook her head.

I took the menu out of her hands and put it to the side with mine. "You don't *have* to eat all of it. I'm going to get the three-meat plate, carne guisada, el pastor, and camaron with rice and beans and flour tortillas on the side. We can share so that you can get a taste of everything. We can get whatever's left over in a to-go box and take it to our room."

"That's so much food. We'll never eat it all." Her frown turned upside down when she saw the drinks coming our way. "The margaritas are huge!"

I gave the waiter our order as Orla sipped her drink through a straw, a smile on her face. There was no more worrying about the amount of food we were getting.

Drinking my margarita, I watched Orla as she looked around at everything. "You seem to like this setting the best, Orla."

"It's so festive. It's sort of like how we do things back home. So much laughter. So much food. So much alcohol. It's what I'm used to. But only on special occasions, not on a daily basis."

As she spoke, I stared at her, wanting to memorize every part of her. I knew I would never be able to forget the green of her eyes. So pale in some ways, yet vibrant in others. Pale green littered with flecks of gold, it seemed that they could go from light to dark and then back again. The smattering of freckles across the bridge of her nose would always make me smile when I thought of her.

When the food came, I enjoyed watching Orla's reaction to each bite she took. Shoving a tortilla chip deep into the fresh guacamole, she sang, "I love guacamole!"

I love you.

Since there was no way I'd be telling her that, I made a note to get her copies of all the recipe books we had for our restaurants at the resort. At least she could do a little Tex-Mex cooking for her family now that she knew how it was supposed to taste.

I took a shrimp off my plate and dunked it into the queso dip. "I prefer this cheese dip to the avocado dip."

She picked up another chip and tried the queso. Another smile lit up her face after she ate it. "Yum. Everything is so good."

Neither of us wanted to completely gorge ourselves, so we got the remainder to go, along with a couple of margaritas, and headed up to our room.

This was going to be it. The last time we'd make love. I didn't know if I even wanted to get any sleep. I just wanted to feel her body against mine all night long.

Orla was all smiles as if she wasn't feeling any of the bittersweetness I was. She danced along the sidewalk to the music we could still hear coming from the Riverwalk. "This has been the best last night, Warner. I cannot thank you enough."

"I aim to please." I had to find a way to pull myself back at least a little. My mind flooded with thoughts about how I could get her to stay. I even found myself wishing she wasn't on any type of birth control, that I could get her pregnant and have her stay with me always. And then I felt very selfish for even having that thought.

She had family back home, and they loved and missed her, not to mention they depended on her to help them out. I, of all people, should respect that, not having parents of my own.

As we got to the room, I put the leftover food in the minifridge. Her hands moved up my sides, and then she wrapped her arms around me, hugging me from behind. "Oh, my prince, this is not going to be an easy night for us."

She'd obviously been holding back the emotions I'd been feeling, not wanting the general public to see her sorrow. "You're exceptionally good at keeping up appearances. I had no idea you were feeling as sad as I am."

"Of course I'm sad, Warner. This is it for us. The last hurrah. Tomorrow morning, we're off back to Austin so I can leave with my group. I'm just practiced at not showing emotion, is all."

I turned to face her, picking her up in my arms. Her feet left the floor as I held her tight. "I'm just not gonna let you go. How about that?"

"How about I stow you away in one of my suitcases?" she asked with laughter in her voice. "We've got to be real here. We knew this day was coming."

"And I think I may have lied to myself about how this would be. I really thought it would be easy to let you go. I honestly never thought I could feel this connected to anyone in only a week's time. Hell, I honestly never thought I could even connect this well with anyone—ever."

"I do think that lots of people have holiday romances. It's common enough. And they leave each other a little richer in experience than they found them." I put her back on her feet, and she ran her hands over my bearded cheeks. "Don't shave this until after I leave."

I moved my hand over hers as she caressed my cheek. "You like it?"

"I love it." She moved her hand back and forth. "It makes you look so rugged and even more handsome. But please shave it off once I'm gone. I don't want to think about you being with any other woman. Let that be my fantasy—that you've stayed single because there was just no other woman who took your fancy the way I did."

"That's what will most likely happen." It wasn't a lie. I was sure I would compare every woman to Orla, and they would all fall short. I felt sure I couldn't make love to her without tears being involved, so I came up with an idea so that neither of us had to see them. "Let's take a shower together."

Blinking, she nodded as she began taking off her clothes. "That sounds lovely."

I went to turn on the water to get it just right and then took my clothes off. She met me in the shower with a sexy smile on her lips. Putting her arms around my neck, I lifted her up, and our mouths came together.

Sparks shot inside of me in all directions as my emotions went on overload. I felt her body shaking as we kissed and knew she was done holding back her emotions. This was hard, grueling, and horrible—anything but easy.

As hard as I tried to push out of my head the fact that she would be gone in less than twenty-four hours, it wouldn't retreat. It stayed right there at the forefront of my mind as we made love.

The water ran over us, washing our tears down the drain, the same way our love was being washed away. Pushing her back against the wall, I thrust into her with such anger that it almost scared me.

I *was* angry. I was angry that life wasn't fair. I was angry that this was the only woman who had ever gotten through the barriers I had put up so long ago—this woman who I couldn't keep.

God had a mean way of bringing people into my life then quickly jerking them away from me. I had no idea what I'd done wrong in my life to become the victim of such cruelty. But whatever it was, I was going to do all I could to change, so I could finally win God's favor and get off this destructive path I'd been placed on.

Gasping with each hard move I made, Orla whispered, "You'll be alright without me. You'll see."

Looking at her, tears moving down my face with the water, I asked, "How do you know that?"

"Because we have to be alright, Warner. We *have* to be."

I wasn't sure that was possible anymore.

20

ORLA

Pulling up to Whisper's Resort before daylight, I knew this would be the hardest day of my life thus far. "I'll go gather my things. I've got half an hour before the shuttle leaves for the airport."

Warner let me out at the lobby doors before he parked his truck in the garage. "I'll be in my office. Come there once you're done."

"Okay." I looked at the truck before getting out, grabbing the *oh shit* bar once more. "I'm going to miss this truck. We've got nothing like it back home."

"It's going to miss you too, baby." Warner sniffed, which I saw as a sign that I should hurry and get out of the truck. If I saw him crying, then I'd start too.

"See you soon." I hopped out and hurried inside, finding some members of my party already sitting in the lobby, waiting for the vans to arrive.

Mona and her mother spotted me right away, as Mona called out, "We were worried about you, Orla Quinn."

"No reason to be worried about me." I headed with purpose toward the elevator. "I'll be down shortly."

Customs would ravage my bags anyway, so I tossed everything into them without care. I put them on a luggage cart, leaving it in the hallway for the porters, who were going around and gathering them, to take to the lobby.

Time was running out. I ran to the elevator, taking it to the ground floor and running out, straight to Warner's office. I closed the door behind me and ran to him, hugging him. I didn't want to let go. I didn't want to leave him behind. "I'm going to miss you so much."

"Keep that picture of us from the Riverwalk on the nightstand by your bed, and I'll do the same with mine." He touched the necklace he'd given me. "And just remember that someone in Texas adores you, Orla Quinn."

"You could come to visit me, Warner." I clasped the diamond-studded Texas in my hand and knew I would never take the necklace off.

I watched his Adam's apple bob as he gulped. "And spend another week or month with you?" He shook his head. "Then have to leave you again? That sounds like torture to me."

It did to me, too. "We have each other's numbers. I think, if either of us gets really bad in some way, we should let the other know, don't you think?"

He nodded. "Yeah. If something horrible happens to me, I'll let you know, or tell one of my brothers to let you know."

"Or something very good too, Warner. We don't only have to share bad news. We can share good news too."

"Please don't call me to tell me that you're getting married or having some other man's baby. I *won't* be happy for you, I can promise you that." He smiled, but I knew he was telling the truth.

And I didn't want to know that about him either. "Deal. No calls with news of that sort. If you feel like there's something you want me to know, then make the call, and I'll do the same."

"We can't have that kind of distance separating us and make things last. We can't fool ourselves."

"Yes, I know. This is it. It's over. No hard feelings. And no sad goodbyes—just as we promised each other in the beginning."

He licked his lips as he gazed down at the floor. "I might not be able to stop the sad goodbye."

I knew it would be impossible. "I'll forgive you if you'll forgive me."

"Deal." He held out his hand as if he wanted a handshake.

I shook his hand, and then he pulled me into his arms again and picked me up, kissing me hard. I held onto him so tightly that I wasn't sure I could let go.

I had truly had no idea this would have happened to us. I thought it would be fun and easy, and no one would fall in love. But even though neither of us dared to say the words, we *had* fallen in love. There would be heartbreak and pain, and there was nothing either of us could do about it.

"The vans are here," I heard someone shout from the lobby.

"Damn it," I cursed. "Why do they have to be on time?"

"Because that's the kind of establishment we run, ma'am." He kissed me once more, softly and sweetly. "Come on, let's make sure you get a comfy place to sit."

We walked at a snail's pace—I was in no hurry to part ways with the man. My hand shook as he held it, walking with me to the waiting van. "Warner, promise me that you'll find someone to love. Your heart is so big that it would be a crime not to let someone in. The way you've let me in." It was so hard to tell him to move on when I loved him so much. But the thought of him being alone made me sick. "Please."

"Shh," he hissed in my ear. "Don't worry about me. I want you to take care of yourself. We can't worry about each other constantly. We have to let each other go now."

"I left the painting that man did of me on Sixth Street in my room. I want you to have it to remember me by it. Don't forget to take it before housekeeping picks it up and throws it away. Don't forget me, my prince."

I thought I might burst at the seams with sadness. Nothing had ever been so hard for me in my life. Nothing at all had come close to hurting me as much as this did.

"My Irish princess, I will never—not ever—forget you. No matter what life has in store for me, you will always live right here," he pressed his hand against his heart, "inside of me. For eternity."

"You are coming, aren't you, Orla?" Mona called out to me.

"I don't want to go," I whispered as I looked into Warner's blue eyes.

"You know you have to." He pulled my hands up and kissed each knuckle. It did little to settle me. "What we had was special."

"What we had was amazing." I took a deep breath and steadied myself. Standing up straight, I shook my head to clear it. "It's been a pleasure in all ways, Mr. Nash."

"Ditto, Miss Quinn." He chuckled. "Everyone's in the van but you."

Nodding, I knew it was time to leave. "I know." I pulled my hands away from his. He held mine so tightly that it made it hard to free them. But finally, I did, and his hands dropped to his sides. "Silly."

"Gorgeous."

"Handsome." I pointed at his beard. "You can shave it off now."

He nodded. "Only for you, my sweet princess."

I backed up until I got to the van and had to turn away from him to get inside. The door slid closed, pushed by a porter. Warner lifted his hand, slowly waving goodbye.

I put my hand to the glass, tears beginning to stream down

my face. I knew this was it—the last time I would ever lay eyes on the man. The tears blurred my vision, and I lost sight of him as we drove away.

An arm came around me, and I didn't even care whose it was. I leaned into their shoulder, sobbing and wishing I hadn't been so stupid as to think that I could do everything I'd done with Warner and not fall in love with him. "I'm a fool."

It was Mona's voice that said, "You're not a fool. You're lucky to have had the experiences you've had with him. And he was lucky to have had you, Orla, even if only for a short while. It's going to be okay. You'll see. You'll both be okay."

I didn't feel like I would ever be okay again. And Mona was the last person I'd ever thought would be nice to me about this. But we came from the same place, and that made us something like family to each other.

Family—the last people I wanted to be thinking of just then. I love my family dearly, but they were the reason I had to let go of the man I love.

But it was the way it had to be.

21

WARNER

Only one month had passed since she'd left, yet it felt as if I'd already spent an eternity without her. I hadn't called her, nor had she called me. We had to let it die out completely, with no hope of resuscitation.

My brother Cohen walked past my open office door. He stopped and looked in at me. "Hey, bro. Some of the other guys and I are heading out to this new club on the southside. You should come."

"Nah." I didn't feel like a night out.

"Why?" he asked as he came into my office, closing the door behind him. "Because you don't look busy. You don't look like you've got anything going on at all. As a matter of fact, when I saw you, you were just staring off into space. So stop sulking over that girl and come out. Join the living, bro."

"It's just that I know I won't be good company. I don't want to get in the way of you guys having a good time. If I come with you, then I *will* be a dud." I didn't believe in putting my sorrowful mood on display either.

"Warner, this isn't you. This isn't the old you or the you that you were when she was around. You're just a shell of a man right now. You need to fill this shell with a new and improved you."

"That's one hell of a yous at one time, bro." I chuckled, and it did feel good to laugh. I knew I had to get out and get over things. There was no use wallowing in self-pity. "Yeah, I'll go with you guys." I got up, grabbed my suit jacket, and followed my brother out.

An hour later, we were sitting at a large table, drinking beer and talking about anything but work. Or they were. I was just drinking the beer and thinking about how I hadn't had an alcoholic drink since the night Orla and I were in San Antonio at the Riverwalk.

"Another round," one of the other guys shouted to the waitress.

I looked around the table and saw that most of the glasses were empty, while mine was still full. Cohen looked at my glass. "Drink up, bro. What're you waiting for?"

"It's been a month since I've drunk anything with alcohol in it."

His eyes got big, and his mouth gaped. "What the hell are you saying to me?"

Lou from accounting answered that for me, "I think he's saying that we need to get him fucked up!"

"Yeah!" all the others shouted and pumped their fists into the air. Some even gave each other high fives over the bad— unbelievably bad—idea.

"No," I said loud enough so they could hear me over their cheering. "I'm not going to get fucked up."

Cohen draped his arm over my shoulders and leaned in close. "I've got an even better idea. We're gonna get you laid, bro. The best way to get over someone is to get over someone else."

"I think you said that wrong. But it doesn't matter. I'm not about to get laid *or* fucked up. I think this was a mistake." I was about to get up when the door to the club opened, and a group of women entered. One of them had auburn hair piled up on top of her head. It caught my eye, and I couldn't stop staring at her.

"Found one already, huh?" my brother asked. "Go ahead. Talk to her."

"First of all, she just walked in through the door. It would be rude to go up to her and start talking before she even gets settled," I said.

Marshall, from housekeeping, nodded in agreement. "Yeah, man. You don't just walk up to a lady who's just come into a club. You gotta grab her a drink first, and then go up to her. But no chit-chat. Just hand her the drink, then start groovin'."

"Groovin'?" I had to ask.

Jones, a porter at the resort, jumped in. Hopping up, he started dancing all slow and bobbing his head a little. "Groovin', boss. Just hand her the drink, then groove a bit before you jerk your head toward the dance floor, and all the rest will fall into place."

"You sure you want to go after another redhead, Warner?" Cohen asked me.

"I don't want to go after *anyone*." They were getting on my nerves, even if they were trying to be helpful. "I'm gonna go find a bathroom."

Getting up, I headed toward the back where the bathrooms were usually found. And just as I saw the sign that said *Studs,* which I assumed meant the men's room, I saw the girl with auburn hair again. She was still with the group she'd come in with. Our eyes met, she smiled and then waved casually.

I stood there, still as stone, as she started walking toward me. I had no idea what to say or do. I felt like bolting. But then she was right there. "Hey there, fella," came her thick accent. It was too thick to be from Texas.

"You from here?" I asked.

"No, sir. I'm from Nashville. Born and raised." She looked back at her group of girlfriends. "I'm down here visitin' my cousin. I ain't never been to this club before. It's cute. I like when they use cool names for the bathrooms. Like this one has studs for the guys and chicks for the girls. It's cute. Don't you think it's cute?"

"You sound like that Miley girl who had a kid's show on television, but then she became a real singer and turned into a slut." I knew that had come out really wrong.

"She's my cousin too," she told me. "I'm a sanger like her."

"You're a what like her?" I really couldn't understand her accent.

"Sang-er," she enunciated. "You know, I sang songs."

"Oh, you sing songs. Okay, I get it now. You're Miley's cousin, and you sing too. You on the radio or anything like that?" I had no idea why I kept up this conversation. I had to believe it was nothing more than that the color of her hair reminded me of Orla's. Because there was nothing else about her that I found attractive—especially not that accent.

"Radio?" she asked as if that was the dumbest question ever. "Gosh, no."

Gosh?

It was too much already. "Sorry. Didn't realize what time it was." I looked at my wrist as if I had a watch on—which I did not. Hadn't worn one in years. "You must pardon me."

"Sure thang, dude."

I walked away and found the guys at my table all looking at me. As soon as I got to the table, Cohen asked, "So, did you score?"

"Um." *Is he insane?* "No. I did not score while I was standing there talking to that girl." I took my seat and downed half the glass of beer, which had gotten warm while I was gone. Another glass sat there waiting for me. I picked it up and took a drink of the cold beer.

"What happened?" Jones asked.

"Well, for starters, she talks like a cartoon character." I took another drink before going on, "And she's that crazy Miley chick's cousin—or so she says, anyway."

Mike, who worked at the front desk, jumped out of his chair, nearly knocking it over. He rushed to the girl I'd just left, and we could hear him from our table. "I love Miley!"

"Okay," I said, then took another drink. "To each his own."

Cohen bumped my shoulder against his. "Come on, bro. You could've given her a better chance than that."

Flabbergasted, I asked, "Did you hear what I said? She said sanger instead of singer. There is no way I could have sex with someone who speaks like that. Can you imagine going down on her—the things she'd say while you were doing it? Well, I can." I did my best to impersonate the accent. *"Garsh, that sure does feel pretty good what yer doin' down there with my undercarriage. It makes me feel like sanging a song fer ya."* They laughed. "And then she'd probably yodel."

They all started laughing while I took another drink and wished like hell that I hadn't let my brother talk me into going out.

If there was something I learned from my night out, it was that I just wasn't ready for this.

22

ORLA

It had been a month to the day since I'd left Warner. I hadn't talked about him with anyone either. But I did continue to wear the expensive necklace he'd given me.

I played with the pendent as I left the bar once my shift was over. Cara, a coworker and old friend that had worked the shift with me, came up to me, taking off her apron. "There's a party at O'Doyle's. Come on, ya can ride with me."

"Oh, no thanks." I wasn't ready to party. I had settled into a fine routine since I'd gotten back. Go home. Read a book. Work on the book I was writing. Go to sleep.

"I haven't seen you out at all since you came back from that trip, Orla. Come on now. You need to get out and see people. And don't try to tell me that you see people each day here at work. It's not the same, and ya know it." She seemed intent on getting me to go out with her.

But I wasn't ready for that. "Look, I'm just not feeling well."

"A pint will cure ya." She looped her arm through mine. "At least come with me for a bit. I hate to walk into places alone. It makes me look like a loser."

I did feel for her on that score and finally agreed to go. "But only for a bit, and only so you don't come off as a loser."

"Thanks, lass."

The smell of beer and cigarettes laid a foul stench on me as soon as we went into the home of Chad O' Doyle. He was known around Kenmare as The Party Man.

He called out a greeting as soon as we came in. "Balls of hay and sausengers on the table. Gurgle, gurgle on the bar. Help yourselves, bonnie lasses."

"Ugh," I huffed as we went to the table. "Bundles of spaghetti noodles and chunks of sausages isn't a meal."

"At least there's beer." She tugged me over to the bar where some bloke was serving up the food. "Can we have two, please?"

"Two gurgle, gurgles comin' up. I'm Tom from London. And you two nice lasses are?"

"I'm Cara, and this is Orla. What has you in Kenmare, Tom?"

"Chad's my sister's ex-boyfriend, and he said I could come visit him anytime I liked. So I came for a visit." He handed me a cup and said, "I like your red curls, Orla."

Tom sported a crop of copper-colored hair atop his round head. For some reason, he combed it straight up, which made him look like the heat miser from that Christmas cartoon.

I just nodded. "Thanks." Sipping on my beer, I looked around the living room to see if there was anyone at the party I might enjoy talking to.

Before my eyes got halfway through scanning the room, John McLemore caught them and came straight to me. "Orla Quinn, it's been a million years since I've seen ya last, ya pretty girl, you."

John was the brother of one of my oldest friends. And he was a bit of a troublemaker—always getting thrown into the clinker for one reason or another.

"Hey, John. How's your family?" I put the plastic party cup to my lips as I continued to look around the room for anyone else who I might be able to talk to.

"Fine. Jules got married last year. Did ya hear about that?"

"I was a bridesmaid at her wedding, John." He'd gotten so drunk at the wedding that he and his father had gotten into a fistfight over it. His father ended up laying John out, and his brothers had to carry him home to sleep it off.

"Oh, yeah. I must've forgotten about that." He held up his empty cup. "I'm gonna get a refill. Care to join me?"

"Mine's full, thanks. But go get yourself one."

"I'll be right back. Don't ya move a muscle, fair Orla."

I made sure to move all of my muscles as I went out the backdoor. I found a bunch of people standing around a fire that burned inside of a metal barrel and walked up to see who was there. "Hey all."

"Orla, that you?" Sean McCallister asked as he came my way. "I haven't seen you around in a long time. What's got you joining us now?"

"Cara." I took a sip as I stepped up to the warm fire. "She made me come with her."

"What has you becoming a shut-in?" he asked as he moved with me.

"I work, Sean. I'm not quite a shut-in."

"Yes, the barmaid thing. Don't you think that you're smarter than that?"

The hair on my arms stood up. I hated when people assumed that what I did was easy, mindless work. "I'm a mixologist. I think that's a pretty prestigious career. And I'm working on a book right now as well."

"A book about being a barmaid?" He chuckled as if he thought himself a comedian.

"A book about mixing cocktails and the origins of each of them. I had some particularly tasty cocktails when I went to

Texas. Some of them were Latin in origin, and some were purely Texan. So I've been studying the history of various liquors and alcohols, and I'm writing a book about that." It was a work in progress, but it was a passion of mine.

"A book about alcohol." He seemed unimpressed. "Who would read that? A drunkard?"

And that's why I don't hang out with old friends anymore.

It always took something to refresh my mind as to why I didn't go to house parties. It was always the same old faces. House parties were always filled with people who hadn't gone anywhere or done anything substantial with their lives.

"It's always a joy to catch up with old friends." I held up my cup, then turned to leave them to their fire and cutting remarks.

"Don't have too much fun, Orla Quinn," Sean called out.

"Not to worry." I headed inside to find Cara and let her know I was leaving. I'd done what I'd said I would, and now it was time to go. I found Cara standing with a group of people and went up behind her. "Hey."

She turned and threw her arms open as if she hadn't seen me in years, instead of only moments. "Here she is!" She pulled me into the circle of people. "This is Orla Quinn, the one I was telling you about. She'd make an exceptional barmaid for your tavern, Mr. Knight."

I looked at the man she'd spoken to and found him smiling at me. He wasn't that old for her to be calling him by such a formal name. "It's a pleasure to meet you, Mr. Knight." I held out my hand.

He took it, turning it over, and kissing the top of it. "The pleasure is all mine," he said with an English accent. "This one has told me of your skillset. I'm in need of a barmaid only a couple of nights out of each week, so I wouldn't be taking you away from your current full-time employment at the lodge. And I would pay you well. My customers are excellent tippers. And

I'm always around the tavern too. We could get to know one another."

If I took the job, I wouldn't have even one night off. "Thanks for the invitation, but I can't take the job. I can help find someone for you, though."

"He likes your look, Orla," Cara whispered in my ear. "He saw you when we came in and asked about you. He's interested in you, silly lass. Don't you get it? In a romantic way."

I didn't like that at all. "Sorry, I can't do it." I spun on my heel and walked out the door without saying another word to anyone.

The idea of another man being attracted to me made my stomach turn. I put my hand around the pendant that hung from my neck. I knew that I didn't belong to Warner Nash. I was free to see whomever I wanted.

But not yet.

23

WARNER

Two solid months had passed since she left and not a day went by that I didn't think about her. Sitting at my desk, eyes on my computer screen, I scrolled through the listings in Kenmare. I wasn't sure what I was doing it for. I just wanted to see what kinds of homes and businesses were available in the town Orla lived in.

Many times, I'd stared at my cell phone, wondering if she was doing the same thing. Too afraid to call, too afraid to hear her sweet voice, I never picked up my phone. I knew it would be too painful for both of us.

But the fact was that the pain of her leaving hadn't gone away yet. My youngest brother, Stone, was the only one of my brothers who told me to listen to that pain. He said it must mean something if it wouldn't go away. My other brothers said to give it time, and it would lessen until there was nothing there anymore.

I didn't know what to do. I had no desire to start seeing anyone else. I had no desire to hang out with people. I felt more alone than I'd ever felt in my life.

Staying home, cooking for myself—alone—watching television—also alone—I had become somewhat of a recluse. I went to work, but as soon as I was done, I left.

The sounds of the busy resort only reminded me of what Orla had said about how things worked in America. How she'd noticed how busy Americans always were and how she thought we should learn to slow down.

I'd even reduced the speed I drove by five miles per hour—which was a big deal for me. The little Irish-accented female voice inside my head would tell me to slow it down, that she didn't want anything to happen to me. And I would do it.

Besides the one night I went out with my brother and the guys from work, I hadn't had another drop of alcohol. I'd moved all the bottles of alcohol in my home into a closet that I'd locked. Seeing anything that had anything to do with cocktails reminded me of her.

The pain that came with reliving the moments with her, knowing they would never happen again, was too much to take. So I tried not to have things around or do things that would remind me of her.

And yet here I was, surfing the internet to see what her part of the world looked like. Often my mind wandered to her and what she was doing. I'd even searched the time difference between us. Six hours separated us. When I came into my office at nine-thirty in the morning, I guessed she was getting ready for her nightshift.

I'd also looked up how long the flight was from me to her. Nine and a half hours. That's all it would take for me to get to her. And I could easily do that. But if I did, then what?

Our lives were still so far apart that even if I could hammer out a long-distance relationship, how much time would we actually get to spend together? And would she even want that?

Looking at a real estate website, I found a picture of a castle for sale. Quickly, I did the calculations to convert pounds into dollars and found it to be staggeringly low for such a place. "Only about six million dollars?"

Scrolling through the pictures, I became more and more excited about this castle. It was surrounded by a moat, which made it look like something out of ancient times. The grey brick structure rose up to five stories, and there was another story below ground. A grotto-style swimming pool was the focal point of a cave-like structure. Soft lights of red, blue, and green came from the rocky ceiling. It was beyond amazing.

Reading on, I found the top four stories each housed a living room, a bedroom, and a bath. The first floor held an enormous kitchen, two dining areas, and two living areas. A wall of windows looked over what the site said was Kenmare Bay.

Tapping my pen to the notebook I'd pulled out of one of the drawers, I jotted down the critical points of the castle. And then I read on to find that the property came with an additional home. A cottage that had been used to house the servants. I wouldn't have traditional servants, so I could make that my home.

Three bedrooms and three baths would be more than enough for me. And then I could turn the castle into an out-of-this-world bed and breakfast.

Who wouldn't want an entire floor to themselves, instead of just a bedroom?

It was a genius idea and one that had to be moved on quickly before someone else snapped up the pristine property. But to make a move like this one, I would have to talk to my brothers and deliver a good and thought out plan as to how I could manage the Kenmare property and still do my job for Whispers Resort.

Bailing on my brothers was out of the question. They counted on me to bring in groups of tourists to the resort. But my heart was leading me elsewhere. I'd never had my heart lead me anywhere, so I knew I had to follow it.

And the castle had almost magically appeared on my computer screen, calling out to my entrepreneurial spirit to make something spectacular out of it.

Looking back at the castle's pictures and the property that came with it, I noticed how there were slopes and small hills. A name came to me—Whisper Hills. I jotted that down and then added—The Castle at Whisper Hills: A Bed and Breakfast Mini-Resort.

Excitement took me over, and I began writing like a madman, tallying up numbers, putting down how many staff members I would need. I developed an entire business plan that day.

And then I called my oldest brother. "Baldwyn, I need to speak with you and our brothers. Can you make it to my place for dinner tonight?"

"Depends on what you'll be serving."

"I'm making barbequed brisket with all the fixings." I was going to butter my brothers up good. All I needed was their blessings to work remotely. But it wouldn't hurt to have their input on the new place I wanted to open in Kenmare.

Later that night, I had all of my brothers sitting in the dining area, and I presented my case to them. I'd brought a television into the dining area so I could show them how grand the castle was. "This is it." I tried not to talk too fast, but I was on pins and needles. "An Irish castle that I'd like to turn into a bed and breakfast. But not just any bed and breakfast—a luxurious bed and breakfast full of history and adventure."

I watched their faces as I went through the pictures, pointing out different things about the property. They listened in silence, which wasn't like them.

By the end of my presentation, I stood there wondering what

was going through their heads. Baldwyn asked, "Are you only doing this so you could be with that woman from a couple of months ago?"

"Not only for that reason." Sure, it was mostly for that reason. Well, it was completely for that reason. But I had to present the business to them, not the relationship I prayed would also come out of it. "I was just scrolling online today, and this castle popped up out of nowhere." I had been on a real estate site, but that was neither here nor there. "And ideas just started coming at me."

Patton frowned. "And what if you do all this and get over there only to find that she's moved on? I mean, I don't know if you looked at this, but did you notice that the castle has been on the market for three years? If you decide you don't want to stay, then it might take a very long time to sell it."

As a businessman, I knew one should never put money into something for personal reasons when it was supposed to be an investment. I took my seat and nodded. For some strange reason, I'd never thought about her moving on.

Now that's all I could think about—*what if she had moved on?*

24

ORLA

I stood behind the bar, stirring a Latin-Irish Rose, a new cocktail I'd come up with. It was a mixture of Irish whisky and rose tequila with a bit of lime juice. It was a knock-off of a margarita, and I served it in a margarita glass with an extra shooter of Patron Silver. Our guests loved it. Placing the finished cocktail in front of the lady who'd ordered it, I smiled. "And here is your Latin-Irish Rose, ma'am."

"It looks beautiful," she said in her American accent. "Thank you, dear."

I watched her as she took her drink and walked away. That accent made my heart ache. I missed him so much—not a day went by that I didn't think about him.

Three months had passed since I'd left. Three months that seemed more like three years. My heart was getting no better. My friends had tried to help me move on, but I just couldn't do it.

No one measured up to Warner Nash—my prince, my cowboy, my lover.

"Good evening, Orla," came a man's voice that I easily recognized.

Turning to find my on-again-off-again boyfriend since high school, I tried to look happy to see him. "Hello, Killian."

"You'd better come out from behind that bar to give your man a hug, lass." He held his arms out wide.

I knew he would come right behind the bar if I didn't do as he asked. So I went and hugged the man I'd hugged many times in my life. "How are you, Killian?"

He held me too long, and I heard him inhaling my scent. "I'm much better now, Orla."

I gave him a gentle push—I wasn't exactly comfortable hugging him like that. "Oh, are you now?" I moved back behind the bar. "And why is that?"

He took a seat, his dark eyes never leaving me. "Because I've missed ya." He tapped the place in front of him. "A pint would be welcome."

Filling a mug with the dark brew, I placed it on the bar. "It's on the house."

With a nod, he lifted the drink to his lips, sipping a hefty amount. Chills ran through me, as I had the feeling that he was trying to build up some courage. And that meant he was about to make a come-on once again.

Putting the mug down, he asked, "Haven't ya missed me at all, lass?"

I hadn't even thought about him in a very long time. But saying that would be rude. "Killian, you seem melancholy."

"Ah, so you have *not* missed your fella, then." He picked up the mug and took another drink.

It was hard to call Killian something as close as a fella or boyfriend. He wasn't one to let me know when he was tired of our relationship and often ghosted me without ever giving me a reason why. "We both know that you're not the boyfriend type. You're a loner—but I don't mean that in a bad way."

"I turned twenty-nine a few months back. Did you know that?"

I hadn't thought about it. "Did you now?"

"And I've been taking stock of my life. It's not looking great at this point." I ran a towel over the shiny bar's surface to rid it of any smudges. He took my hand as it came near him. "I'm lonely."

I moved my hand, not falling for any of his antics. "Who isn't?"

"You and I have chemistry."

"If our chemistry was so good, then why did you keep leaving me?" I raised one brow as I looked at him for his answer. He'd never given me even one speck of information on this subject.

He couldn't look me in the eye and looked down at the bar instead. "I was afraid of how I would begin to feel with you. And that had me leaving ya. I was afraid of falling in love with you, Orla Quinn." He looked up at me. "I was afraid of that because I knew you weren't falling in love with me."

How right he was. "I'm sorry for that, Killian. It may have been my fault the first time. But the other times, it wasn't. When you left me the very first time, I lost the ability to fall in love with you for fear you'd leave me again. So we're both to blame for the lack of love in our relationship."

Nodding, he seemed to accept his share of the blame. "But we're grown now. And we've finally been honest with each other—which is new. I can't stop thinking about you, Orla. I think it's a sign that we should try one more time to make things work between us. I think you might be the one for me, mot."

Closing my eyes, I knew that I didn't want the man who sat in front of me. I wanted Warner. But I couldn't have him.

Will I die sad and alone because I won't let go of the man I cannot have?

I wasn't ready to date, much less have a relationship. And Killian seemed to want the kind of relationship that would end in marriage. "Look, I'm not sure what to say to you."

"Say that you'll give me one more chance to show you that I can be the man you deserve. I'm working with my father in his groundskeeping business now. He's styling me to take over once he's ready to retire. One day, the business will be mine. And any successful man needs a good woman behind him. You're that woman for me, Orla."

"You've been bouncing from job to job for years, Killian. How can you expect me to believe that you'll stick around for this one?" He was asking for a great deal of trust from me.

"This will be *my* business one day, Orla. Why would you think that I would leave it? You act like you don't even know me." He took another drink as he scowled at me over the rim.

I didn't really know him. I knew many things about him. But I didn't know who he was when he disappeared from town. "And how would I know you when you've left me high and dry so many times?"

His eyes drooped at the outer corners. "Will you ever let me live that down, lass?"

If he didn't like hearing the truth, he shouldn't have sought me out. "Look, Killian, I'm not the same person I was when you and I were together. It's been over a year, and I've changed. I'm not about to beat about the bush, trying not to hurt your feelings. I'm into being honest and real with people now. And honestly, I don't know you anymore."

"I've changed too, ya know." He huffed, puffing out his chest. "You're not the only one who can grow as a person."

The one thing I could say about Killian that I couldn't say about any other man in Kenmare was that I did have a past with him. I did know him better than I knew any of my past boyfriends—save Warner.

At the thought of the man, I found myself shaking my head. "I'm not at a place in my life where I feel that I can give my all to you, Killian. So I'm sorry, but you're wasting your time with me."

"Please, Orla. Please, give me a chance to show you that I'm not the same man you knew back then. I'm no longer the irresponsible, selfish man. But you won't know that if you don't give me a chance. Give *us* a chance. Please."

How can I do that when my heart belongs to someone else?

But I'd have to give someone a chance eventually, wouldn't I?

25

WARNER

It took several months for the purchase of the castle to go through, but the paperwork was finally done, and I was on my way to it—at last. Six months had passed since I'd last seen Orla.

I rented a car and drove the fifty miles from the airport to Kenmare. Driving on the wrong side of the road wasn't nearly as hard as I had thought it would be. But the only cars they had at the rental agency were tiny. I felt like a clown in a minuscule car after driving tall trucks for most of my adult life.

I'd almost called Orla with my big news but decided not to. I wanted to see her face when she saw me. I had made one call, though—to the bar where she worked. I had to make sure what time she'd be there so I could surprise her.

Even if she had gotten herself a boyfriend, my hopes were that I still held the majority of her heart, and she'd leave him for me. It was selfish of me, I knew, but at least I owned that negative aspect about myself.

Although all I really wanted to do was find Orla, I had to take care of business at the castle first. I'd had the real estate agent hire a temporary assistant for me. He'd handled hiring the head groundkeeper, and the two of them were in charge of hiring a team of people to work under their supervision. We'd scheduled a meeting that morning, so I could meet everyone and let them know the game plan for the business.

There was more hiring to be done, though. I would need a chef and kitchen staff. I would need an event coordinator, too, as we'd decided we wanted to offer the place as a wedding venue.

I'd had the grotto bar stocked prior to my arrival and planned on asking Orla to run it for me. I wanted her to manage any and everything to do with the bar. I'd come prepared to offer her much more money than she was already making. I would double, even triple what she'd been making to get her to come work with me.

A small part of me was afraid that she would turn me down, especially if she were currently seeing someone. But I'd made the decision, before I even began negotiating to buy the castle, that I was doing this for me above all else.

I'd been drawn to here for some reason. Perhaps it was for Orla, or maybe it was for something else. Whatever it was, the pull was strong, and it wouldn't let up.

It felt to me as if fate had a hand in what was happening. I had to let go of the reins and let fate lead me to where I was supposed to be. And it helped that my brothers finally agreed that I should follow my heart, as I'd had it closed off for nearly all my life.

The navigation system took me right to the castle's gates. A wall of the same grey bricks used to make the castle's exterior walls ran around the property, except where it met Kenmare Bay. Large iron gates kept people from driving in without permission.

I rolled down the window and pressed the call button on the keypad. "Whisper Hills," came a woman's voice. "How can I help ya?"

"This is Warner Nash, the owner."

"Oh, yes!" she said with excitement. "We've been expecting ya, sir."

The gates began to move, each one sliding into the walls on the sides. I liked the way it looked. I'd had the road repaved to be sure it looked new for the guests I would soon have. The road wound through the small hills and shallow valleys, all the way to a drawbridge.

My heart raced as the drawbridge was lowered, and I felt as if I'd stepped back in time. I kept the window down as I drove over the wooden bridge. Looking out the window, I glanced down and saw the rust-colored water. It filled a moat that went all the way around the castle. It was an extraordinary place that I knew people from around the globe would want to come and see for themselves.

We still had to work on the finishing touches, but I had wanted to be a part of it. Then, when we were done with those, we'd put the site online and begin marketing it. I already saw so many things I could take pictures of to put on the site.

As I drove off the bridge, I found myself in a parking lot that had room for about twenty or so cars. I drove right up to the front entrance, amazed at seeing it in person.

The pictures had been nice, but they hadn't shown its grandeur. Two imposing fifteen-foot high wooden doors stood before me. Large loops of bronze metal made up the door handles, and there was a long rope on the right side of the doors. I pulled the rope and heard the beautiful sound of bells going off inside the stone walls.

The door opened, and a plump woman with grey hair wearing a grey dress with a full, white apron curtsied. "Master Nash, I'm Grace O'Malley, your head housekeeper. It's a great pleasure to meet you, sir."

I chuckled, as hearing myself called Master Nash seemed incredibly ridiculous. But it would sound great to the guests—

add to the history of the place. So I didn't correct her. "Grace, it's a pleasure to meet you as well."

She stepped back and drew back her arm. "Please come in and take a look at your place, sir."

The foyer was dimly lit, and the stone walls shone with what looked like moisture. I had to touch it, as I thought that would only result in mold and mildew if it stayed that way. I found it to be dry, though. "Are these walls painted to look wet?"

"Yes, sir, they are," Grace told me. "This castle has been updated many times throughout its history. With central heating and air, all the drafty areas had to be sealed. This place is airtight now."

I'd been told every feature and aspect of the home and had it in writing as well. While it looked like an ancient castle, it had all the things people expected something new to have. Everything had been modernized while keeping the old-world charm. It was a masterful combination, and I looked around in awe.

We'd made a deal to keep all the artwork, furnishings, and decorations the previous owner had left. I was glad to have done that, as it made the place feel just right.

As Grace led me through one of the living areas, she said, "The rest of the staff is in the large dining room. I took the responsibility of making something to eat and drink for the meeting. I do understand that you will be hiring kitchen staff."

"I will be doing that very soon." Stone had offered his help in finding me a great Irish chef. He'd already narrowed it down to three men and a woman, and I would interview them soon to find who would work best for me.

Stepping into the dining room, I found everyone standing up. One of the older men came up to me with his hand extended. "Hello, Mr. Nash. I'm Callum Sullivan, your head groundkeeper. It's nice to finally meet you."

"You too, Callum." I looked at the others and waved. "Hi.

Nice to meet you all. I won't keep you too long. I just wanted to introduce myself and let you know that I'll be a hands-on owner who will also be managing things here. So you'll be seeing a lot of me, and I'll be seeing a lot of all of you. My brothers and I own a resort in Texas, and we treat our employees like family, so expect no different from me here. Let's all respect each other and help one another out when we can, and I think we'll all get along perfectly."

One of the housekeepers raised her hand. She was young but not shy at all as she asked, "Does everyone in America speak the way you do—with that accent?"

"No," I said. "No, they don't. I'm from Texas—born and raised there, so I've got a distinctive Texan accent. There are quite a few distinctive regional American accents, so I can't say that there is any one type of way we sound. Hopefully, you'll get to hear a lot of them once we open for business."

"I can't wait! I'm Darleen, by the way," she said before sitting down.

"Nice to meet you, Darleen." There was a lot to do, and I wanted to get started, plus I wanted to see my new home at the other end of the property. "I'll be ordering name tags for everyone because that will make it easier on our guests. We'll all get the chance to get to know each other in no time at all. For now, I'll let you get back to work while I go see my new home."

Getting back into my car, I drove along another winding road to the cottage. When I saw it for the first time, I felt a spark. Again, the pictures I'd seen hadn't done it justice.

This was no quaint cottage; this was a sprawling home with remarkable flower gardens surrounding it. I had to fight myself not to run around like a little kid to see what I would find.

Small statues of fairies and elves peeked out from behind the flowers and bushes. It was beyond adorable, and I knew in an instant that Orla would fall in love with the place.

As I opened the door, a rush of emotion came over me. "This is home."

I stepped inside and instantly fell in love with the place. This was a real home. Everything had been left behind, and the things I'd sent over had already been put away, I found as I made my way through the house.

My things were in the master suite, clothes hung in the closet, t-shirts, underwear, and socks in the drawers, all neatly put away. And the bathroom had all of my toiletries too.

I went from one room to another, finding each one different. My room was done in soft greys and deep blues. The next room was done in bright reds and soft grey accents. And then I opened the door to the last bedroom—a nursery.

My heart sped up as I imagined my future here. It was perfect.

26

ORLA

Cara arrived for her waitressing shift just as I came in to tend the bar. She bumped her shoulder to mine as she caught up to me. "So, how's it been goin' with old Killian? It's been about three months now, hasn't it?"

It hadn't been bad, but it hadn't been amazing either. "It's okay. He's been very busy tending to the groundskeeping business, as his father took on a job as head groundskeeper for some rich guy. It's all top secret from what Killian's told me. His father isn't allowed to say where he's working or who he's working for."

Cara put her apron on, then ran her hands over her straight blonde hair to ensure it was all smoothed out. "I heard that Mr. Knight—you remember, the Englishman who owns that tavern that you ran away from like a child—"

"What about him?" I interrupted. I knew who she was talking about.

"I heard he's bought an estate. I bet you that's who Killian's father is working for. That man is extremely secretive for some reason."

"Something about him made me feel a bit scared, to be honest with you. It wouldn't surprise me a bit if he bought himself some creepy place to take women so they could play those BDSM games." I shuddered as I went behind the bar and put on an apron.

"Anyway," she said as she sat at the bar. There were only two guests seated at the bar, so she had the time. "You never answered my question. How's it goin' with Killian?"

"Like I said, he's busy." I still hadn't let him come over to my place yet, and he wasn't happy about it. "He's sort of frustrated with me because I haven't had sex with him yet."

Her brows rose in surprise. "And why haven't you done that?"

"I just don't know about him yet. He's run off on me so many times that I can't find it in myself to trust him fully. And I'm not about to have sex with a man I can't fully trust." I didn't have the heart to tell Killian that I still held another man in my heart and that that was the real reason I hadn't had sex with him. Even kissing him felt wrong, so there was damn little of that as well.

"You know, I don't think you're giving that man a proper chance to win your affection." She nodded at me as if she could see right through me.

I knew I wasn't. "Look, it's just not going to be that easy for me to fall in love with him. We've got too much history for me to forget what's happened in our past. At least, not for some time. I suppose he'll have to prove to me that he's not going anywhere before I can let my guard down with him again."

"He's a cutie, you know that, right?" She winked at me. "Many a girl wants that man. And if you won't give him the affection a man needs, he's likely to find it elsewhere."

Not even a hint of jealousy flared in me at the thought. "If that's what he wants, he's free to go for it. Who am I to stop him from searching for love elsewhere?"

"I thought you were his girl? He calls you that. And what do you call him, Orla?"

"I call him Killian. When I'm talking about him to someone, I say Killian this and Killian that. I don't call him *my* anything. And that's because he's *not* mine, and regardless of what he calls me, I'm not yet his anything either. But I am giving him the time and the chance to prove he won't run off again. And, in time, that may be enough to allow me to open my heart to him." At least I knew that my heart could open up. It had with Warner.

"I hope he'll wait that long for you, Orla. I truly do. I think that man is going places in his life now that he's being groomed to take over his father's business—they're doing very well right now." She winked at me. "You could do worse, you know."

I knew one thing for damn sure. *I can do better, too.*

I hadn't told anyone about my time with Warner. The people who'd gone on the trip with me knew about it, especially the people who I'd ridden with in the shuttle. They'd seen me crying all the way to the airport, wailing like a banshee about my heart feeling as if it was being ripped out of my body. But they'd been nice enough not to go about town talking about what a fool I'd been to hook up with the resort owner.

No one I worked with knew about Warner. And if I had my way, none of them ever would. I had a hard enough time keeping that man out of mind as it was. I didn't need anyone else bringing him up.

"I've gotta get to work, Cara." I turned away from her to begin polishing the glassware. "These glasses aren't going to clean themselves." I was done with the conversation anyway. I didn't need to hear how wonderful Killian was or how many girls would love to be in my place.

Those girls never had to wait for a phone call that never came until the moment they finally got over him. Killian had always seemed to have an abnormal sense of timing—as if he exactly knew when I'd moved on or forgotten about him. And that's right when he would show up to win me back. And that had worked for him time and time again.

By God, it's working for him even now!

Somehow, he'd made me feel guilty about not giving him one more chance. I'd caved and told him that we could see how things went. He'd been patient with me, and that was something new.

As I rubbed a tall glass with my white bar towel, I thought about how much Killian had truly changed. He wasn't a totally new person, but he had grown up enough in the time we were apart that it made a difference. And then I wondered about how he instinctively knew when I had put him out of my mind.

We must have more of a connection than I thought.

If there were no connection at all, I wouldn't have cared if he was sad or not. I wouldn't have cared if he wanted another chance with me. He *had* grown as a man. I could see that clearly now. He'd found patience. He'd found commitment. And he'd even found trust.

I was the one who hadn't found any of that for him. I'd only felt guilt. Maybe I was just as much at fault for all the breakups after all. It may well have been my guarded heart that had kept the love from developing in our relationship.

I'd blamed him for so long for running away that I must not have looked at my part in how things had played out.

He always came back to me. He always knew when my heart was heading in another direction. And that could've only come from a real connection. One he recognized, and I was blind to.

And more than that, Killian was actually here. He was here, and he wanted to be with me. And I couldn't say that about everyone.

27

WARNER

After a shower and putting on a nice suit—I'd checked out the website for Orla's resort, and it was pretty ritzy—I was on my way in my tiny rental car to see it. Finally, after six long months.

The wait was over. I no longer had to sulk about because I would never see her again. I no longer had to agonize over how I would never hold her in my arms again. I would no longer have to try to find my place in a future without her in it.

At least that's what I hoped.

There were no guarantees that she'd want me. Her heart had been open when she left, and some other man might have been able to slip inside of it while I took my time coming to my senses on the other side of the world.

A lot could happen in six months. A person could fall in love and get married in that time. If she were married, I would have to accept it. My plan of stealing her away from a boyfriend was one thing. But I wouldn't want to break up a marriage.

I took in a sharp breath as it occurred to me that she might even be pregnant by this hypothetical man she'd married. "God, no!"

If I'd waited too long to get to her, I would kick myself in the ass. If she was so far out of reach that it would be impossible for us to ever be together, I didn't know what I would do.

I'd been telling myself that I'd come to Ireland for myself. But now, as panic rushed through me at these thoughts, I knew that wasn't entirely true.

I wasn't drawn to Ireland. I was drawn to Orla.

My brothers would be so disappointed in me if nothing came of this entire endeavor. It would be better if they were mad at me over it; I could handle their anger much better than I could handle disappointing my family.

Even with all the doubt, I had to see her. I knew where she was, and I had to see her. I couldn't turn around and go back to Whisper Hills without finding out if there was a chance in hell for us to get back to where we were before she left.

The lights of the resort shone in front of me. It was a beautiful sight, glistening like a beacon in the night. The place looked inviting.

Pulling up to the valet, I got out of the car, trying not to look as if I was about to puke. "Nash."

The man wrote that on a tag and then said, "Enjoy your evening, Mr. Nash."

I headed inside, my entire body hot with nausea. A herd of pterodactyls moved in waves around my stomach. Beads of sweat popped out of my forehead, and I knew I had to get to a bathroom—and fast.

I saw a sign that said *Gents* on a door in the lobby, and I made my way to it as cool and casually as I possibly could. Heading inside, I found it wasn't a private bathroom as I'd hoped. Anyone could walk in on me at any time. I went into a stall and took deep breaths. "Stop being so afraid."

So many thoughts kept popping like popcorn in my head, and not one of them had a positive energy about it. Everything had headed to a dark place. She was married. She was pregnant with another man's child.

I heard the door open and held my breath. I didn't want anyone to see me in my present state. I knew I was sweating profusely, and I was sure I'd gone pale too.

I heard the man turn on the water—it sounded like he was splashing himself, and I overheard what sounded like a pep talk. "Get it together, man. You love her. You always have. You can do this. She needs you to do this so she can feel safe about loving you," he said.

I stepped back, and my foot hit the metal trash can, sending it crashing to the marble floor with a terrible racket. I knew I had to come out of the stall now, or I'd look like a real weirdo.

As I opened the stall door, I felt my cheeks burning with embarrassment. "Sorry about that. I kicked over the trash can." I went to wash my hands, trying to act cool.

"So, ya heard me being an idiot, did ya?"

"Hey." I held my hands up in the air. "No judgment here, bro. I've been talking to myself all damn day over a woman."

"So I'm in good company then." He pulled a little black box out of the pocket of his slacks. He wasn't wearing a suit, the way I thought a man who must be on the verge of proposing would. Especially in a place like this. Instead, he wore tan slacks and a cream-colored sweater. His shoulder-length hair was dark and on the unruly side, and his eyes were dark with thick, matching the brows above them.

"Seems so." I ran my wet hands over my face. "Think she'll say yes?"

"I'm really not sure." He put the box back into his pocket. "We've got a long history, but she's not coming around the way I thought she would. I'm hoping that making a commitment to her in this way will help see that I'm in it for the long haul."

"I wish you luck, man." I hoped giving some other guy a bit of luck would help with my karma.

"Are you here to see a woman too?"

"I am. I haven't seen or spoken to her in months, and she has no idea I've come to Ireland. I have no idea what will happen, and I'm nervous as hell."

"Ah, you love her." He nodded knowingly.

"I do."

"Ya, I love my girl too. But I'm not positive that she loves me."

"Mine used to love me, I do know that much. The real question is, does she love me still? And is she free to start seeing me again?"

"Well, good luck," he said. "I've got to face my challenge now."

"No time like the present." I looked back into the mirror. "I've gotta clean up a little before I head out there."

"See ya." He left me alone, and I took several more deep breaths before feeling somewhat confident enough to go out there and find her.

With my head held high, shoulders back, I walked out of that restroom with a confidence that I didn't entirely feel. But they always say to put on the face of the man you want to be. Or some shit like that.

Spotting the sign above the bar, I went in through the open door—and stopped in my tracks. My heart stopped, and so did my breathing.

The man I'd met in the restroom was on his knee, the black box in his hand, and standing in front of him was Orla.

I'm too fucking late.

28

ORLA

Cara's eyes went to the door of the bar. "Were you expecting Killian to come in tonight, Orla?"

"No." I turned to find him smiling at me.

It had been a couple of hours since I'd had the epiphany about my share of blame in our breakups. And now here he was. The man really did have perfect timing—just as I had been thinking earlier. *That must mean something, right?*

"There's my love." He came to the bar, reaching over it to pull me to him and leaving a light kiss on my lips.

I waited to feel them tingle the way they did when I had kissed Warner, but there was nothing there at all. I hoped that could be attributed to the fact that I hadn't actually let the idea of my culpability really seep into my heart and mind yet.

Surely the spark will come in time.

But we still had plenty of time to see if something could build between us, now that I'd become aware of our connection. "What are you doing here, Killian?"

"You. As always." He took my hand, and his eyes glistened. "Take a break." He seemed to be giddy, and I had no idea why.

"Okay, I'll take a break." I looked at the other barmaid. "Can you deal with things for fifteen minutes or so?"

"Sure thing, Orla. Take your time."

Taking off my apron, I left it under the bar and walked around it to find Killian's arms wrapped around me. "Thanks, mot."

I didn't wrap my arms back around him instinctively, the way I'd done with Warner. It made me feel terrible how guarded I'd kept myself with Killian. Slowly, I moved them to hug him back. "It's really not a problem to take a break, but you're welcome."

He moved me back to take a seat on one of the empty bar stools and then stood in front of me. "How's the night been goin'?"

"Good." I wasn't sure what he was getting at. "Would you like to go out later or something? Is that why you're acting so strange?"

"I'd love to go out later." He beamed with happiness.

Damn, I've been a real bitch. This man clearly adores me.

"Then we can go out after I get off." I patted his hand, as he hadn't let mine go. "I'm sorry if I've been putting you off."

"You are?" His dark brows rose, and he looked at me in a way that made me think he was about to cry. It only made me feel worse.

"I *am* sorry for how I've been treating you—keeping you at arm's length all the time. I'm going to try to stop doing that to you."

"I do love ya, you know." He took both my hands in his as he looked into my eyes.

I looked back into his and tried to feel a spark. But nothing happened. "I believe you."

It wasn't what he'd hoped to hear—the way his face fell told me that much. "In all these years, you've never loved me, Orla?"

I wasn't sure if I'd stumbled upon love or not. "Killian, I'm not sure what I feel for you. But I have come to realize something important. I haven't been letting you into my heart. It's not the way I've seen things in the past. By continuing to guard my heart, I shut you out. And now that I've realized how I hurt our relationship in the past by being closed off, I've got some things to think about."

"You have no idea how good it is to hear you say that, Orla." He stepped back. "And I've got something I'd like to say too. I think what I have to say might help you better understand me and how I feel about you—about *us*."

It boggled my mind how I hadn't seen how the man looked at me before. He absolutely adored me, and I'd never even noticed. It made me angry with myself.

Here I was, perfectly able to open my heart to a man I'd known only a couple of days. I'd fallen head over heels in love with a man who was really a stranger to me.

And here was Killian. I'd known him forever, and we'd begun our romance back when I was in my teens. Yet, I had never opened my heart to him. Not in all the years that he kept giving me a chance after chance to do so. I'd never let myself love this man who so clearly loved me.

"I've been so blind to you, Killian." I reached out and ran my hand over his smooth cheek. He'd never grown a beard. I had loved Warner's beard.

Warner? I have got to stop thinking about him. What's wrong with me?

I had a perfectly good man standing right in front of me, and there my mind kept going back to Warner and how wonderful things had been with him. I couldn't keep comparing my interactions with men to my ones with Warner when sparks would fly every time we slightly touched.

If I was going to move on with Killian, I had to let Warner go. I had to really leave him behind. A person can't move on while they're carrying a ball and chain around their heart.

I reached up and grasped the necklace Warner had given me. I never took it off. Not even to shower.

For six months, that necklace had been my connection to Warner. I knew that I had to take it off, or I would never move on. I would become a lonely old spinster—just me and my necklace to remind me of a love that could never be.

I felt someone push my shoulder from behind, and then I heard Cara whispering, "Are ya blind, lass? He's on one knee, he is."

Blinking, I looked down to find Killian smiling up at me. "Orla Quinn, I'd like to ask you a very important question."

My hand held the Texas-shaped pendent, not wanting to let it go. My heart stopped beating as I watched Killian pull out a small black box from his pocket. He flipped the lid open, and there was a small gold ring with a solitary diamond on top of the band. The light hit it, and it glistened as if trying to capture my attention.

I broke into a sweat, knowing exactly what this meant. *Say yes to him, and we can stay together. Say no to him, and he will end things with me for good.*

"Orla, I know you don't think I'm stable or committed to you. But with this ring, I want you to understand the level of commitment I am willing to give to you, my love. Marry me. Marry me, and I'll make you happy for all our days. I swear this to you. Orla Quinn, will you do me the great honor of becoming my wife?"

My jaw felt tight. My mouth wouldn't open. My hand wouldn't move away from the piece of jewelry I clung to. I looked up, away from Killian for a moment, to try to get my bearings and gain some wits about myself.

A man was standing in the doorway across the room. His

mouth hung open, and there was a pain in his blue eyes. More than pain—agony—in a pair of eyes that were so familiar and dear to me.

This cannot be real.

"Warner?"

29

WARNER

I was finally able to take a breath when she said my name. She hadn't answered the man's proposal. "Yes, it's me, Orla."

She looked down at the man I'd met in the men's room, her hand still wrapped around the necklace I'd given her. "I'm sorry, Killian."

He stood and then turned to me. Confusion was quickly replaced by recognition as he looked at me. "You?"

I nodded. "Seems so."

"*You* are here for *my* woman?" he shouted as he slowly began moving towards me.

"She's not yours yet, by the sounds of it." I didn't want to be cruel, but I wasn't about to step back and give him room where she was concerned.

"She would be, had ya not come through the door." He moved a bit faster, still headed in my direction.

I had the feeling he intended to fight me. "Look, I don't want trouble. I came here to speak to Orla."

"She doesn't need to hear anything you have to say," he roared and charged right at me.

I was ready to take on the man and squared up in anticipation of his attack when Orla was suddenly in front of me. "No, Killian!"

"Get out of my way, woman!" I watched as he threw out one hand, trying to push her out of the way.

I wasn't about to let him touch her that way. I quickly grabbed her by the waist, picking her up and moving her behind me. "I've got this, baby."

"No!" She screamed as she pounded on my back. My body nearly filled the doorway, trapping her in the hallway behind me where she would be safe. "Warner, don't fight him!"

I hesitated for a moment, not understanding why she didn't want me to fight him. *Unless she's in love with him.*

Dropping my fists, I turned to her but wasn't able to say a word as the man came up behind me, grabbing both my arms and pulling them behind my back before dragging me across the floor. "You get away from her!"

"Killian, stop that right now!" Her hands went to her hips, and her jaw turned tight. "This is enough!"

He let me go, and the two of us stood there, looking at her. I was pretty sure that neither of us was sure who she loved at that point. And neither of us knew what to say either.

A blonde woman came around in front of us, looking back and forth between us. "Night and day, they are." She looked at Orla. "So, you found a fella while on holiday, did ya, lass? You kept that a secret, didn't ya?"

"That she did," the man growled as he stepped up next to me.

Orla's hand once again went to the Texas-shaped pendant I'd given her. It made me wonder how often she'd held it that way in the six months since we'd last seen each other. "Killian, I'm sorry. I'm a bit confused right now." Her eyes came to me. "Why didn't you call to tell me you were coming, Warner?"

"I wanted to surprise you. I've got so much to tell you, Orla."

The way her eyes sort of bugged out told me she wasn't happy with my surprise. "Warner, you should've called."

"Sorry."

"Did you thought that my life wouldn't go on without you?" she asked with a tremor in her voice.

I didn't want to make her cry. "Orla, it's not that at all. I just missed you so much that I made some decisions. I had no idea if you'd moved on or not. But I didn't want to sit back and wait to find out."

"She moved on," the man standing next to me said with what sounded like gravel in his voice.

"Have I, Killian?" she asked him.

He looked at her, and I saw the pain in his dark eyes. "Haven't ya, mot?"

I couldn't help but smile a bit—he'd called her that dreadful term of endearment. She preferred being called baby, and I knew that for a fact. "Have you moved on, baby?"

"You two need to stop." She stepped out of the doorway and pointed at the exit. "You two need to leave right now. I'll have no more of this. I have to think about things."

"Orla," I pleaded. "You have to talk to me. I have so much to tell you."

"Warner, do not test me right now. You've no idea how easy it would be for me to unravel at this moment."

She'd reached her breaking point, and I had to step back. I took one of my new business cards out of my wallet and placed it on the bar behind me. "You can reach me at this number when you're ready to talk."

Nothing was going the way I had thought it would. No joyous reunion. No hugs. No sweet, sweet kisses. But still, I wasn't unhappy about having come to Ireland. There was still hope. I just had to have a bit more patience.

Killian led the way out of the place, and we ended up in the parking lot together, both of us looking uneasy. I had no idea how close she was to him, and he had no idea how close she was to me.

I thought it time we both found out. "Look, let's start over, Killian. I'm Warner Nash." I held out my hand to shake his.

He looked at my hand for a long moment, then finally shook it. "I'm Killian Sullivan."

"Sullivan?" I asked. "A man named Callum Sullivan works for me. Is he any relation to you?"

"He's my father. So, you're the rich bastard he's been working for. Why'd you swear him to secrecy over who you are and where he's employed?"

"I didn't want Orla to find out that I was coming." What an incredible coincidence that I'd hired the father of the man who sought to take my girl. "So, she never told you about me?"

"She never told anyone that I know of ya." He grinned. "Guess that's cause she meant to leave you behind–*completely*."

"She never told me about you either. She said she'd had some insignificant relationships in the past, nothing serious, though. Did you two meet in the last six months?"

"She's been my girl since the tenth grade," he informed me.

"Constantly?" I did recall her saying something about an on-again-off-again thing she'd had with one guy.

His confident grin vanished. "Not constantly, no."

"And you two got back together when?"

"We've been together for the last three months."

I felt something in my gut twist like a knife. The thought of her having sex with anyone made me crazy with jealousy. "Intimately?" I didn't want to know and had no idea why I'd asked that question.

"As if that's any of your business," he barked.

"No, you're right, it's not." I did find his answer slightly off, though. If they had been having sex, he would've lorded that over me—I was sure of it.

If they hadn't been together that way in three months, then there might still be hope for me.

30

ORLA

My body quaked with what I could only assume was shock. "Cara, I've got to get out of here."

"Lilith," Cara called out to the other barmaid. "Orla's out for the rest of the night. The bar is yours." She came to me, wrapping her arm around my shoulders. "Come on, doll. I'll drive ya home. You're in no condition to do it yourself."

"Thank you, Cara." I *was* a mess.

"I'll grab our things and meet you at my car." She let me go, and I began making my way out of there.

Going to the staff parking lot, I prayed that I wouldn't find either man waiting for me. I hoped I'd been stern enough that they both understood that I was in no condition to deal with either of them.

Getting into Cara's car, I thought I might cry for a moment. By the time she slid in behind the steering wheel, I'd managed to suck it up. She tossed our things into the backseat, then started the car and took off. "You've got a real pickle on your hands, Orla Quinn."

"I know." Not that I knew what to do about it.

"Were you and that America guy really that close?"

"I've never been closer to a man in my life." I knew that was the truth. I was confused about a lot of things at the moment, but not about that.

"You were only away for a week," she reminded me. "You couldn't have gotten closer to him than you've gotten with, say, Killian? You've known Killian practically your whole life! You two have been an item since we were in high school."

"But we've never been very close." Gulping, I tried to force down the knot that had lodged in my throat. "I loved Warner."

"Phppt!" She made a silly sound. "How in the world do you think you fell in love with a man you only knew for seven days?"

"I don't know how it happened. But it did." And I was sure he'd fallen in love with me in that short amount of time too. I'd known it before, and I knew he wouldn't be in Ireland right now if that weren't the case.

"But you just had that breakthrough about how you feel about Killian," she reminded me. She seemed to be exceptionally good at recollecting things I'd told her.

"Yes, but that breakthrough wasn't that I loved him. It was about trying to take a better look at the connection we share—one that I might've been blind to. And the thing is, maybe only Killian has a connection to me, but I don't have one to him. I don't feel the same spark that I feel with Warner. I don't feel any spark with Killian. I never have."

"I can see why you have sparks with that Warner fella. He's hot. And he looks rich as sin, too."

"He *is* both." I bit my lower lip as I had a brief memory of our sexual escapades. "And he's the most amazing lover I've ever had."

"To be fair," she said, "you haven't had sex with Killian in over a year. How can you be sure that *he's* not the most amazing lover you will ever have unless you give him a shot at showing you?"

I found my hand once again wrapped around the pendent that hung in the space between my breasts, directly over my heart. "I can't do it, Cara. I can't bring myself to be with Killian like that. I can't bring myself to be with anyone like that."

"Not even Warner?" she asked with one raised brow.

"I'm in shock right now. I can't feel much of anything." I didn't know what I would and wouldn't do at that point. "I don't know if I can let myself to do anything with Warner—it's been six months, and I haven't been able to get over him. And that after we'd only been together for a week. If I start it all over again, it may take my entire life to get over him. I can't do that to myself."

"What if he's here to ask you to marry and wants to take you back to America with him?" She asked. From her perspective, it was a valid point.

But I knew he wouldn't even think about doing that. "He knows how I feel about that. I've got to be here for my family. And he's got to be in Austin with his brothers and the resort they own. I don't know why he thought coming for a visit was a good idea."

"Well, to be fair, you don't know why he came."

Nodding, I knew there were things I had to talk to Warner about. But I knew that I couldn't trust myself to be alone with him. "I've got to build up some sort of wall around my heart before I see him again. I can't talk to Warner unless I can keep myself from doing something that would hurt me in the end."

"You have no idea how long he'll be here, though. How long will ya wait to talk to the man?"

"I have no idea." *Maybe it would be best not to talk to him at all.*

"This is just my opinion, and I know I haven't found the man for me yet, but I'm going to say this to ya anyway as it's burin' a hole in my heart not to. You have yet to get over Warner. You still love him; I can hear it in your voice. And the way that man looked at you told me that he loves you too."

"So does Killian," I whispered, guilt filling me to the brim.

"But *you* do not love Killian," she stated.

I do not love Killian. I love Warner.

"I still don't know what to do. Warner will leave, and Killian won't."

"Yeah," she agreed. "I'm just guessing here, but you and Warner didn't do an official breakup when you left, huh?"

"No, we did not break up, but I guess we were never really together. I mean, we were *together,* but we knew the whole time that I had to leave. It was a tearful goodbye, too. I cried all the way to the airport. And then I cried off and on throughout the entire flight. Although I'd learned how to cry quietly by that time."

"You've got to get closure with Warner. You have to talk to him and tell each other that it is over and done with. Maybe then you can both move on."

"You're right. If I have an ending for Warner and me, then I might be able to move on. And I might find that I could let Killian into my heart. Or I might find that I cannot let him in, and I'll end things with him as well. Either way, I've got to move on with my life." I'd been treading water, so to speak, for too long now. It was time to make a change. Maybe even more than one.

She pulled up to my cottage and parked the car. "Should I come in, or would you rather be alone?"

"I've got some crying to do," I admitted. "This shook me to my core. I'd be dreadful company right now, but thank you for the offer, and thanks for the ride home. You're a true friend."

I grabbed my purse from the backseat and went into my home. As I tossed the purse onto the table by the front door, some of the things inside spilled out.

Picking them up, I wondered why my purse was unzipped in the first place. I was sure I'd closed it. A small card lay on the table, and I remembered why it was open. Cara had picked up the business card Warner had placed on the bar, and she'd put it into my purse before bringing it out to the car.

The card had a picture of a castle on it. *The Castle at Whisper Hills, Bed and Breakfast, Mini-Resort.* There was a local phone number too. I'd never heard of this place, but the castle did look familiar.

Ah, the one that's been for sale on the bay for the last few years.

But what did it have to do with Warner?

31

WARNER

I didn't get much sleep on the first night in my new home. Not that it felt uncomfortable to be there, but it felt uncomfortable not knowing what Orla was thinking or what she was going to do.

Interrupting a marriage proposal wasn't exactly how I thought I would find her. But now I knew there was another man in her life. And that left me extremely uncomfortable.

After getting dressed, I went to the castle to better familiarize myself with the place. I'd been in such a hurry to go see Orla that I hadn't even taken a tour of the castle before I had left the evening before.

No one had come to work yet, so I was all alone in the castle. Just as I'd come in through the front entrance, I heard a buzzing sound, and I followed the noise until I arrived to a box on the wall. It seemed to be an intercom system, so I pressed the button at the bottom of the box. "Yes?"

"Warner, is that you?" came Orla's voice.

I felt like I might fall down, I was so relieved to hear her voice. "It's me, Orla. Are you at the gate?"

"I am. Can you give me the code to open these gates?"

I saw another button on the box and pushed it. "I can do even better for you." I pushed the button. "Are they opening now?"

"Yes. Thank you. Where are you?"

"I'm in the castle. Just follow the road to the drawbridge. I left it down, so you can drive right over and park near the little car that I'm renting. I'll meet you there."

"Okay. See you in a minute or so then."

I ran around like a chicken with my head cut off as I searched for a mirror to make sure I looked okay. Finally, I found one and ran my hands through my hair before running out the front doors.

Panting with excitement, I knew I had to calm down. I had no idea what she was here to tell me. I couldn't get my hopes up too high, or it would be devastating if she had bad news for me.

Her car was as tiny as mine was, I noted as she parked next to my rental. "Do they even make average-sized cars in this country?"

I went to her as she got out of the car. All I could think about was holding her in my arms and kissing her sweet lips. But she held up one hand. "No hugging."

Immediately the air left my lungs. "I'm glad you came."

She looked up and down at the castle behind me. "What's with this? And why is it called Whisper Hills? Did you and your brothers buy a freaking castle?"

"Come inside. Let's talk in there. It's foggy out here." I led the way back inside. "Is it always so foggy in the mornings here?"

"Yes." She followed me inside. "This place is gorgeous." She shook her head as if to clear it. "You didn't answer my question."

"I bought this place." I watched her reaction as I took a seat on a nearby sofa. "Please, have a seat anywhere you like."

She took a seat across from me. "You bought this place? And you're going to be running a bed and breakfast here? Or you're just here to get things set up, and then you'll be leaving?"

"I'm here to stay." I kept my eyes on hers to see what she thought about that. "I am making Kenmare my home."

"And your home in Austin?" she asked without giving away any reaction whatsoever.

"I still have it. I'll have to go back there each quarter for meetings, and I'll stay in the house when I go. But most of the time, I'll be here, in Kenmare, managing this business."

Uncertainty shined in her green eyes. "So, you are *not* leaving?"

"I am *not* leaving."

She looked at her hands, which she'd been wringing in her lap. Smoothing them over her slacks, she asked, "Why did you come here, Warner?"

"For you, Orla." There was nothing else I'd come for but her. I knew that without a doubt now.

She blinked several times as her jaw hung open. "You came here, bought a castle, and are about to start a business, and you did all of this for me?"

"I did. And I want you to be my partner in this business. I want you to manage the bar and maybe some other things here, too. Fifty-fifty—what do you say to that?"

"I say that I'll have to think about it."

"You will become a very rich woman if you take the offer."

"I'm not quite understanding you. You came here, got this castle, are turning it into a business, and you want me to own half of it? Is that right? You came to give me something that will make me wealthy?"

"No." She wasn't understanding me completely. "That's a by-product of why I came here. I came here for *you*. I came here because I love *you*. I came here because living life without *you* doesn't make me happy. I came here because I missed *you,* and not a day has gone by in these last six months that I have not thought about *you*."

"This is overwhelming."

I got up and went to her, taking her hand. "Come with me. I want to show you something."

She came along without any hesitation. My hand burned where it touched hers. The electricity between us was still there, strong as ever.

I took her to my car and then drove her to the cottage. It wasn't as glorious-looking in the fog as it was in the sunshine, but I did see her eyes widen when she saw it. "What's this?"

"This is my new home. I'll be renting out the rooms at the castle. But this will be home." I got out of the car, and she did too, meeting me in front of it. I took her by the hand again and took her inside.

"This is lovely, Warner."

"Look around. I'm going to go get something, and I'll be right back."

I wasn't going to waste another minute. I got the item I'd bought for her before leaving Austin and took it to her.

She was in the kitchen, marveling at everything. "This place is five times the size of mine. And it's beautiful. Everything is new in here. Top of the line appliances, too."

I took her by the hand again, leading her back to the living room to stand in front of the fireplace. The flames crackled, and the light from the fire made her glow like the angel that she was.

Her eyes darted back and forth as I got down on one knee and held out the ring that I'd bought for her. "I know you've got one proposal on the table already. And I am not asking you this just to one-up Killian, I swear that to you. I bought this ring before even leaving Austin. This had always been my intention, Orla."

I held the ring between my thumb and forefinger, holding it

out to her. Her hand trembled as she stretched her fingers out, moving them toward the ring. "You came here to ask me to marry you?"

"I did." I'd had this lengthy proposal planned out. But it didn't seem to matter now. "I love you more than I knew possible, and I want to marry you. I want to make you happy, and I want you to make me happy. I want us to be partners in every way imaginable, baby. Become my wife, and I will become your husband. We can build a family together. All you have to do is say yes."

She looked away from the sparkling ring and looked into my eyes. I don't know how much time passed as we stared at each other—it could have been ten seconds or ten minutes. All I knew was that my heart stopped beating as I waited to hear the most important word of my entire life.

"Yes." Tears flowed down her cheeks, and soon my eyes were stinging as well.

"You have no idea how happy you've just made me, baby." I slid the ring onto her finger, and the tears spilled over.

Finally, we'll be together forever.

EPILOGUE
ORLA

Six months later

Breathless, I clung to my husband's shoulders as he thrust into me so hard that the bed shook each time. It was the night of our honeymoon, and we'd taken the top floor of the castle as our suite for the night.

Consummating the marriage, we made love with more than one mission that night. Now that we'd committed to a future together, starting a family was our top priority. Making each other happy was a close second.

Perhaps it was the nursery that had already been set up in the cottage that made us feel such an urgency to fill it with our first baby. We were prepared to make love like rabbits until we became pregnant. And I was overjoyed at the idea.

Warner's lips pressed against the side of my neck, then he grazed his teeth down, leaving a trail of lava behind. "Yes, babe," I hissed. Every time his mouth touched my neck, it drew passion out of me in abundance.

I wrapped my legs around him, arching my body up to meet

each savage thrust. He bit my earlobe, and his hot breath tickled my ear. "No. Call me what you did at the end of the marriage ceremony."

"Yes, my husband." I moaned as he grabbed one of my legs, moving up so that my knee was next to my head. He plunged even deeper inside of me.

"My wife," he groaned. "My Irish princess is now my queen."

"And my prince is now my king." I raked my nails along his back as my body began to shake with a need to release.

My body called out for more from him. He gave me more, and then even more than that until I screamed. My orgasm took me on a journey to a place only he and I could find together.

He followed me on the journey, moaning his release. And then his mouth was on mine, kissing me harder, still thrusting, so the orgasm went deeper.

With no other thoughts but of pleasing him and being pleased by him, I fell into an abyss of pleasure and knew it would always be this way.

Our love would last. And we would leave a legacy behind us for our children and grandchildren, and their grandchildren as well. Not only had we formed a union in marriage, but we'd also formed a business that would see our children through a profitable future.

Life was good, and it was only beginning. With love, respect, and an insane connection, the Quinn-Nash family would be long-lived. And nothing would make me happier than that.

～

Warner

Two months later

"Orla, honey, where are you?" I called out as I walked into the cottage.

"I'm back here," I heard her say.

Going down the hallway, I found her sitting in the large white rocking chair in the nursery. Rocking back and forth, she had a smile on her face.

I knew, instinctively, that she had some news for me. Walking to her, I got on my knees in front of her. "Tell me."

"Tell you what?" she teased me.

"I want to hear you say it, wife." I took both her hands, making her stop rocking. "Tell me."

"I don't know what you mean." She giggled as her green eyes sparkled with happiness.

She delighted in teasing me as much as I did her. We made perfect business partners as well as perfect partners in marriage. I knew we would—never had any doubt at all. And I hoped we were about to partner on a new venture.

"You most certainly do know what I mean. *Our* plan. Has it come to fruition?" I had to know. My patience had never been worse.

"Our plan?" she asked with a whimsical note to her voice. "What plan would that be? The one about having a Christmas party out here for the town of Kenmare? Because I haven't finished the math on that yet. The Irish can drink, and I'm not sure we can buy enough Guinness to quench the whole town's thirst."

"We *can* buy enough for that. And that's not what I'm talking about, and you know it." I pulled her hands up and kissed each knuckle one at a time. "I will give you a thousand pounds if you stop playing around, and just tell me already."

"As if I need your thousand pounds. My accounts have never been so full. Money isn't the way to get me to talk, Mr. Quinn-Nash."

"Ah, but I know what will." Jumping up, I scooped her out of the chair and kissed her sweet lips until she panted with desire. "Tell me, Orla Quinn-Nash. Tell me the words I've been waiting an eternity to hear come out of your perfect, sexy mouth."

She looked into my eyes, and I watched as hers began to shimmer. "Warner, are you sure that you're ready?"

"I've been ready."

"My dear husband, you are the light and love of my life. You are the yin to my yang. You are both the sun and moon to me. And it is my distinct pleasure to give you this news. All of our hard work has paid off."

"It has?" My legs began growing weak, and I sat in the rocking chair, holding her on my lap.

"You'll be a daddy in about eight months. We'll be parents."

Pressing my forehead against hers, I whispered, "Now you've done it, wife. You've gone and made me even happier than I knew I could be."

And I think we have found our happily ever after.

The End

www.ingramcontent.com/pod-product-compliance
Lightning Source LLC
LaVergne TN
LVHW021711060526
838200LV00050B/2607